HAUNTINGS

from the Snake River Plain

River St. Press
Twin Falls, Idaho
riverstpress.com

River St. Press

Other books by River St. Press

VOICES FROM THE SNAKE RIVER PLAIN

BILLIE NEVILLE TAKES A LEAP

HAUNTINGS

from the Snake River Plain

Copyright © 2014 by Bonnie Dodge and Patricia Santos Marcantonio

All rights reserved. Without limiting the rights under copyright reserved above, no part of this publication may be reproduced, stored in or introduced into a retrieval system, or transmitted, in any form or by any means (electronic, mechanical, photocopying, recording or otherwise), without the prior written permission of the copyright owner and publisher of this book.

Second Edition Hauntings from the Snake River Plain

ISBN-13: 978-0692243060
ISBN-10: 0692243062

LIBRARY OF CONGRESS CATALOGING IN PUBLICATION DATA
Hauntings from the Snake River Plain / edited by Bonnie Dodge and Patricia Santos Marcantonio
1. Ghost stories - Idaho. 2. Hauntings. 3. American literature. I. Dodge, Bonnie. II. Marcantonio, Patricia Santos.

Published in the United States of America
Set in Book Antiqua

Publisher's Note
Many of these selections are works of fiction. Names, characters, and incidents either are the products of the authors' imagination or are used fictitiously, and any resemblance to actual persons, living or dead, or events is entirely coincidental.

River St. Press
P. O. Box 5073
Twin Falls, ID 83303
riverstpress.com

INTRODUCTION

Everyone is haunted by something. A dead mother's voice. The howl of a dog abandoned in the desert. A doorbell ringing at midnight. The scent of lavender hanging in the air.

You don't have to walk through a cemetery to be haunted. All you have to do is look at pictures of relatives, or recall something you love, long for and miss. Maybe it's the town you grew up in. Maybe it's your grandmother's smile, or one of Creedence Clearwater Revival's songs playing on the radio.

As River St. Press one of our goals is to encourage others to share their stories. Our call for ghost stories was met with tremendous enthusiasm, resulting is this delightful anthology.

Whether or not you believe in ghosts, we know you are going to enjoy this collection from writers on the Snake River Plain. In these pages you will encounter haunted houses, canyons and ballrooms, to name only a few of the stories included here for your pleasure.

Lock the doors. Turn on all the lights. Pull up a chair and enjoy.

Bonnie Dodge
Patricia Santos Marcantonio

CONTENTS

INTRODUCTION i

LOST SOULS OF THE LOST CAVE
by Andrew W. Black 1

UNIVERSITY INN IN GOODING, IDAHO
by Patricia Santos Marcantonio 9

THE MYSTERIOUS VISITORS
by Linda Helms 11

UNREST
by Bill Cope 19

POSSESSED
by Bonnie Dodge 29

SHOSHONE INDIAN ICE CAVES
by Patricia Santos Marcantonio 37

INCIDENT NEAR SUCCOR CREEK
by Maggie Koger 41

AUNT EDDIE
by Jay Michaels 45

HAILEY'S RIVER STREET
by Jo Ann Robbins 49

PETROGLYPHS
by Patricia Santos Marcantonio 53

THE HAUNTED FIELD
by Cathy Wilson 65

GHOSTS OF THE CANYON
by W. Lenore Mobley 69

BILLY
by Bonnie Dodge 77

CONTENTS

JUMPING THE GUN
by Conda V. Douglas — 81

THE HAUNTING OF ROOM 10
Soloaga House in Shoshone, Idaho
by Karma Metzler Fitzgerald — 91

THE WINNEBAGO PHANTOM
by Sherri George — 95

NIGHTHAWKS
by Grove Koger — 105

SPIRITS OF THE OLD STATE PEN
by Patricia Santos Marcantonio — 109

SCHUBERT THEATER IN GOODING — 113

THE BLIND MAN'S DOG
by Giselle Jeffries — 115

DEAD MAN'S SHOES
by Patricia Santos Marcantonio — 119

SCALLOPED EDGES
by Sherry Schubert McAllister — 133

FACES IN THE WATER
by Patricia Santos Marcantonio — 143

STRANGER IN A SNOWSTORM
by Loyd Bakewell — 151

PIECES OF HEAVEN CUPCAKERY
by Patricia Santos Marcantonio — 157

TWIN FALLS' GHOSTLY LIBRARIAN
by Bonnie Dodge — 161

WHERE STORIES ARE BORN
by Nadine York — 163

THE SPIRIT IN THE BASEMENT
by Eileen Davidson — 173

SHADOWS AT THE SIDEWINDERS BAR
by Patricia Santos Marcantonio — 179

CONTENTS

SPIRITS OF THE SUMMER OF LOVE
by Elaine Ambrose — 181

THE DOG CAME BACK
by Kathy McIntosh — 191

HOW TO OUTSMART A GHOST
by Loy Ann Bell — 199

LINCOLN SCHOOL'S WOMAN IN BLACK
by Patricia Santos Marcantonio — 209

LINGERING IN SILVER CITY
by Bonnie Dodge — 213

SARA'S HOUSE
by Cheryl Maude — 219

UNSETTLED SOULS IDAHO CITY CEMETERY
by Patricia Santos Marcantonio — 229

EPOCH IN A DRY AND THIRSTY LAND
by Vaughn Phelps — 233

DAKOTA FRANDSEN
by Patricia Santos Marcantonio — 241

LIVING ON THE LAKE
by Patricia Santos Marcantonio — 245

A GUARDIAN GHOST
by Judy Ferro — 251

THE SPIRITS OF STRICKER RANCH
by Sherri George — 255

WHERE GO THE GHOSTS?
by Bonnie Dodge — 259

ABOUT THE AUTHORS — 261

PHOTO CREDITS — 268

LOST SOULS OF THE LOST CAVE
by Andrew W. Black

The old adage goes "curiosity killed the cat." I can't help but smirk at that ironic truth.

My name is Edward Pinkerton. Before you brush this off thinking it nothing more than the overly dramatic ramblings of a young inexperienced explorer, know that I began my career shortly after the Great Depression and am nearing retirement. I should amend that I "was" nearing retirement. My expeditions ranged from the ruins of Peru's peaks to the deepest pits of Africa and beyond. A veritable treasure hunter and thrill-seeker am I, and have never experienced anything truly eerie or peculiar. Until my latest travels across the Atlantic where I ran into a group of Uncle Sam's boys. After sharing rounds and conversing for a time, I learned one of the soldiers was from a place called Idaho. He told me of a collection of seldom-visited Lost Caves strewn about the desert between Boise and Pocatello. For someone looking for a new and interesting exploit, this seemed the greatest of coincidences.

Once my foreign business was concluded, I set out for the rock and sage of Idaho's flatland. I began my search outside the Capital finding some larger and unfortunately well-visited caves. Though I did not find the adventure I was looking for, it gave me the opportunity to learn what I could expect to find in future caves. Erosion played a small factor in the formation of many of the caves. Most were the result of either volcanic activity creating flow tubes, or by the motion and flex of the Earth's plates. Still, these caves lacked that "untouched" character I longed for. So I elected to renew my search in a less populated area.

Visiting each rural town, I inquired into the prospective caves, and began to fear that soldier sent me to a lost cause rather than an actual lost cave. I had nearly given up the endeavor when I came to the town of Eden. After many inquiries, I finally heard of a cave in the desert to the north.

Little was known about it except local superstitions and rumors of people who went missing inside. However, the area and lack of credible information promised that this one was mostly unexplored. Eventually, I found a local cattleman who showed me the entrance he referred to as a snake hole he tried to keep his smaller cattle away from. My path set, I prepared to delve its depths the following day.

Curious how utterly ordinary my final day began. Starting with a brisk morning breakfasting of eggs and bacon, nothing foreshadowed the horror I would soon face.

I typically explored with at least one other person for safety, but out of eagerness as well as perhaps hubris, I decided to not seek out a local to join me. Carrying a small pack with canister lights, chalk, canteen, a kerosene lantern, and a notepad in my pocket, I arrived at the snake hole by late morning, hoping the summer sun would have already enticed any such creatures out of this den. Once I was sure the way was clear, I began my descent through the cave opening — just large enough for an average man to squeeze through. I crawled through a short tunnel and came to a twenty-foot drop. I lowered my pack with a rope I had already anchored outside the tunnel and rappelled down.

I was struck by how dark it was so near the entrance. A canister light in hand and my pack reset about my shoulders, I began my trek down the main chamber. The cave was a three-tone world, the yellow of my light to the gray of the rock and the black of the shadows.

Lost Souls of the Lost Cave

At first I had a moment of disappointment, when heading down the main tunnel, I saw modern markings designed to help previous visitors find their way back out. But I pressed on in hope that I could find a path not taken. Much to my delight, I came to the end of the main passageway where a great many other chasms and caves branched off. I concluded the tunnels leading upward would either come to an abrupt end or alternate entrance, so I focused my attention on the lower ones. The best thing about these chambers was that I could see no markings, which I hoped meant they had not yet been explored.

One tunnel, darker and deeper than the rest, called to me. Now, in my paranoid state, I wondered if it was my own conscious and inquisitive thought I heard beckon, or some insidious external voice. With ne'er a second thought, I chalked my route and plunged into the black depths. Climbing over protruding boulders and crouching under low craggy ceilings, I marked my return path, while dreaming of discovering long lost primordial hieroglyphs or a giant deposit of rare minerals.

After what seemed like two hours, I stopped to change out my second dimming canister light and rest. Sitting on a large rock, I surveyed the surrounding rock that sparkled either from water condensation or a reflective mica-type mineral mixed into the dull dark gray of the common stone. But something in the corner of my eye turned my gaze. Directing my light down the tunnel I was headed, I saw a flicker of movement. At first it looked as though the shadows themselves had moved. I doubted an animal or person could be down this far, but still listened for any sound of life.

The silence was overwhelming. My ears hummed, rejecting the sheer inaudibility of the place. Deciding my own mind toyed with me in the eerie seclusion, I stood and began making my way back, watching for my markers.

I hurried along and wondered how far I had traveled. Every corner, every rock, every marker appeared the same as the last. I panicked when my third light dimmed as I tried to grasp how much farther I had to go. I was down to my last canister light and lantern. Worse still was the unsettling sensation that the shadows behind me were consciously following, as if they were more than disembodied absence of light. In this entire trek back, I had not come across an alternate route or adjoining chamber, yet I was certain during my ingoing voyage I had encountered many.

I felt I was going in a circle in one large endless tunnel. In an attempt to put my nerves at ease, I drew a large ring on the wall of the cave. If I didn't come across it again, I'd know I wasn't going in circles. Assuring myself I would not see it, I walked on. In no more than ten minutes, I came to a stop in front of my mark. Only this time it seemed dull and faded. Perhaps I had lazily sketched it or the moisture had caused the chalk to not stick. But to my already fraying state of mind, I imagined something had tried to remove it and now that chalk mark was a loathsome symbol of my failing predicament. Motion again alerted me to my dark pursuers. I rushed down the tunnel, climbing and crawling to get away from the darkness that peered hungrily at my back. In my terrified state, I stumbled and fell, dashing my last fully charged canister light upon the rocks.

As the filament of the bulb faded away, I became enveloped by a world of endless stone and an eternal black realm where the only remaining sense was touch.

Bellowing like a child, I tore into my pack trying to get a dim light to fend off the darkness I felt grab hold of my ankle. With one such light, I burst the glow in the direction of my assailant. The shadows retreated, but to a short distance.

Lost Souls of the Lost Cave

Though it could have been my waning light was pulsing with low energy, the mass of darkness seemed to bulge and shrink like a giant chest heaving with excitement. Glancing at my ankle, I noticed a stone had rolled onto my leg. I would have questioned my sanity if not for the innate instinct, the unknowable truth that the blackness was in some way alive and sought to extinguish me. My only salvation was in the light. I quickly grabbed my remaining source. How the lantern survived my fall I know not save for a cruel means to give me hope.

The orange light of the lantern flickered to life as I got to my feet once again. I waved the light to and fro as if to cause discomfort to the surrounding shadows. I continued on my way in a final effort to escape this prison of rock and endless night. At last, I came across a branching passage that had to have been my exit after traveling in an endless tunnel for what felt like days. My heart rushed with excitement at the prospect of freedom and life. Seeing what looked like the way up, I ran to the tunnel's end only to find a wall from floor to ceiling. Overwhelmed, I fell to my knees.

These pages cannot adequately express the horror. Even as I sit and write, I see clearly now the shadowy forms in the dark, perhaps spirits of the missing or entities of a more sinister world. I am certain I need not worry about starvation or exposure, but my death will come when the last flame goes out.

So with the last of my light and final moments of life, I waste no time on prayers and hopes or a farewell to loved ones. Instead, I tell my story and offer a final message.

If by some means my tale reaches the surface, do not discard it as a simple ghost story. Stay clear of this place. My footsteps lead only to death and despair.

If you are a fellow unfortunate who has stumbled upon

whatever remains of me and find yourself in a similar situation, I wish you a more swift and peaceful death than I fear I shall receive.

I bid you welcome, fellow lost soul of the lost cave.

UNIVERSITY INN IN GOODING: WELCOMING GUESTS AND MAYBE SPIRITS
by Patricia Santos Marcantonio

The large building at the edge of Gooding has lived many lives.

Gooding College operated there from 1917 to the late 1930s. At one time, the campus included eight buildings. When the college closed, the site became the state tuberculosis hospital, serving patients of all ages from the late 1940s until it closed in 1976.

The remaining building was called Tenney Hall during the college days and housed the TB hospital nurses and doctors. It was turned into a bed and breakfast in the early 2000s. The building is now owned by Daniel and Svetlana Brown, who operate the University Inn and Resort.

The 19,000 square-foot structure is made of light sandstone and brick and includes a welcoming porch. But the building is known for more than its history.

Among paranormal investigators and local residents, it also may be home to spirits. People who have stayed at the inn reported hearing furniture move in Room 210, although nothing was out of place, Svetlana said.

Her daughter also has heard marbles rolling down the hall and in the morning, found a marble on the floor of the hallway. Another woman reported that someone or something moved shiny black half-marbles from the top of a plant all over the building. Svetlana said she has even found them in the hallways and on top of picture frames. All the paranormal action seems to take place from three to five in the morning.

Ghost hunters have conducted several investigations at the building. HauntedPlaces.org reported apparitions of an old man in a white coat and a woman with a young girl, along with sounds of whispers and footsteps from empty hallways.

In a 2008 *Idaho Magazine* article, the former building owners talked about several strange occurrences. Once, when they checked on their fussy young nephew, they found him asleep. The crib sheets were tucked underneath like hospital corners and a comforter placed over the boy. They also said a CD player turned on when it was shut off, and a ball rolled through their living room and they didn't know who rolled it. Their visitors were convinced the former hospital was haunted by the souls of the doctors, nurses and patients.

Like the former owners, Svetlana Brown has yet to see any apparitions, and only one of their guests was wary of the supposed haunted residents. "Most people who stayed here like it," she said.

The Browns may be too busy remodeling the building, which they also rent for reunions, to worry about ghosts. In the meantime, Svetlana is not bothered by the possibility of spirits sharing the space with their large family.

She said, "It's just a home."

THE MYSTERIOUS VISITORS
by Linda Helms

I heard water running but no faucets were on. Then I heard voices near the back porch. "Hello, who's there?" I called from the kitchen. No answer. I stepped onto the porch. The sink was dry. No one was in the backyard.

I'm Sally Russell, retired from teaching sixth-grade English in Helena, Montana, for twenty years. They were good students, but I wanted more time to pursue other things in life.

My college friend, Rachel, who lived just north of Jerome, Idaho, invited me to look at property there. In June, I bought Mr. Jefferson's old house with five acres of pasture and moved in. What intrigued me most were the thick rock walls. The house must've been built in the early 1900s with the basalt rock of the area where mostly sagebrush grew.

The house had two bedrooms, a parlor, and an L-shaped kitchen. A long screened porch ran across the entire back of the house with a bathroom off the porch. Under the porch was a basement, and west of the house an old wooden shed and rock barn. The place had not been lived in for several years.

I cleaned the house, the yard and garden over the next three weeks. I repaired the fence lines before putting my quarter horse mare into pasture. I heard voices and running water several more times during the week. Still, no one was there. No water was running. Maybe I had left the garden hose on or the stock tank water.

Buster, my cocker spaniel, an inside dog, loved to be outside while I worked in the yard. One evening while I was listening to the radio in the kitchen, Buster's ears perked up and he emitted a low growl. He slowly crawled to the back porch. I followed and peered into the yard. I didn't see anything. Maybe a neighbor's dog or perhaps a skunk?

In the morning, we walked towards the garden past the shed. Two empty Mason jars sat on a bench, which I had not noticed before. I left them there and went on with my yard work while Buster chased butterflies.

During the night, I again heard voices and water running. This time, lights flashed in the yard. I walked carefully to the back porch and shined my flashlight, but did not see where the lights came from. The sound of water was gone.

The next morning, I walked to the bench for the jars, thinking they would make a nice flower decoration for the kitchen. They were not there.

Buster had an appointment with the vet. Afterwards, I stopped at the assessor's office to find out more about the house. The assessor asked if I knew about the trouble the original owner had in the 1920s. He suggested stopping at the historical society museum. There, a volunteer showed me a notebook full of information about all the rock homes in the county. Mine was the first one in the book and listed on the National Register of Historic Places. On the computer, she also found that Joe Marsh, the owner in 1920, got caught making and selling moonshine from his home. In 1942, another owner, Ralph Steele was killed in the basement, but the murder was never solved.

I told my friend Rachel there might be ghosts at my home. I explained what I had seen and the information I got at the museum. Now a paranormal investigator, Rachel came over that evening just before sunset. We sat in the dark at my kitchen table waiting for something to happen. We were ready to give up, when, just before midnight, Buster growled. I quieted him. In the moonlight, a faint outline of a tall slender

The Mysterious Visitors

man stepped out of the shed. Moments later, a shorter, heavier shadow of a man appeared in the driveway carrying a flashlight and two empty jars. The figures went into the shed.

I looked at Rachel and whispered, "Did you see that?" She nodded. We waited a few minutes more, and they both walked out. This time, the taller figure carried the two jars, as if they were full of something. The shorter one still held the flashlight. They walked toward the front driveway and disappeared into the darkness.

I whispered to Rachel, "What do you think?"

With a short chuckle she said, "Oh, you have spirits here all right. But I don't think they will do any harm. Do they ever come to the house?"

"No, but sometimes the water faucet on the porch sounds like it's turned on."

"In my experience, as long as they don't invade the house, you should be OK. In the morning we'll check out the shed." The next day, we found footprints in the doorway.

"This is a new one for the books," Rachel said. "Usually, apparitions don't leave footprints. Maybe there is more to these ghosts than we thought. Let's do some more investigating."

We met at the museum the following afternoon. A newspaper article stated the men arrested in 1920 for moonshine spent thirty days in jail and were never seen again in these parts. We also found something interesting in the oral histories of area residents. Another owner of my house, Mrs. Sanders, told about two men coming into her yard July 10, 1932, while she and her young son worked in the garden. Her husband was in the shed. The men went into the shed and opened a long wooden box in the corner. Her husband asked, "Who are you? What are you doing?"

"We're just here to get our stuff." The men picked up a

metal cream can and a gallon wooden bucket that they carried out the door. They disappeared around the corner of the highway leading to the canyon. Later, the sheriff explained that the men they had seen lived there ten years before, but had died. The tall, thin man, Joe Marsh, died in a Pocatello hotel the day the family saw them at the shed, and Fred Strong died in a Boise hospital three weeks prior, both from natural causes. Mrs. Sanders called it a mystery.

Now, there were two mysteries—the moonshiners and the murder. Were they linked? Rachel and I wanted to know more about the murder in July 1942 to see if that was the case.

At the museum we found Ralph Steele's obituary in a 1942 newspaper. A newspaper article reported no leads to the perpetrator, but a coroner ruled Steele had probably been beaten to death on July 10. His body was not found until three days later by his son who lived in Hailey and had come to visit. On the Internet, we discovered Steele's grandson had the case re-opened in 1982. Apparently, no one went into the basement after Steele's body had been found until the grandson and his private investigator did. The suspected murder weapon, a hickory baseball bat, was in a corner of the dirt floor under an old rolled up rug. What appeared to be dried blood and hair on the bat was analyzed for DNA. It matched hair from a brush belonging to his grandfather. Also, fingerprints on the bat matched those of Joe Marsh, the moonshiner who had died in Pocatello ten years before the murder.

"Since the investigation has anyone cleaned or remodeled the basement?" Rachel asked.

"Yes," I replied. "I found out the previous owners cleaned and poured a concrete floor. They put an overstuffed chair, desk and small bookshelf down there. Books would be removed from the shelves and left on the couch or desk when the owners weren't there. They would put the books away

The Mysterious Visitors

and two or three days later, different books would be out. This happened several times over the next month. After the owners moved, the house reverted to the bank. When I moved in, the basement furniture was still there, but no books."

Rachel looked concerned. "Even though you haven't noticed any apparitions in the house, you might watch for something in the basement."

"I guess I should. I haven't been down there since I moved in."

Although the mysteries were still unsolved, I spent the first week of July pruning bushes, picking cherries, and making needed repairs.

One afternoon during a light rainstorm, I decided to take a better look at the basement. I opened the door and Buster started down the wooden steps ahead of me, but stopped halfway and growled. I heard what sounded like a book fall to the floor. I switched on the light and picked up a book in front of the chair. *The Poetry of Edgar Allan Poe*. An envelope was placed in the middle. I opened to that page and found the poem, "The Raven." The envelope was addressed to Mr. Ralph Steele at my address. The postmark was Pocatello, July 5, 1942. A paper inside had these words: "July 10 is the deadline." It was signed, Joe.

I drove to the sheriff's office. He volunteered to check for fingerprints and DNA. A week later, the sheriff dropped by with the results.

"You won't believe what they found. This note was sent by the same Joe Marsh who killed Ralph Steele."

After the sheriff left, I said, "This has got to stop here and now. I can't have a ghost in my house." I opened the basement door, turned on the light, and walked to the bottom of the steps.

"Joe Marsh, I know who you are and that you want to

live here. You can have the basement if you promise to never show yourself anywhere else in the house or on my property."

Back at the top of the stairs, I put a note on the basement door and locked it. "Joe Marsh's private quarters. Do not enter."

There. I hoped he would honor my request.

On July 10, I walked to the mailbox. Along with the usual junk mail, bills, and a letter from my cousin in Colorado, there was an envelope with no return address, postage stamp or postmark, addressed to me. Inside the mysterious envelope was a note similar to the one addressed to Ralph Steele.

I smiled as I read. "July 10 is the deadline. Quoth the Raven, Nevermore. Thank you. Joe."

UNREST
by Bill Cope

"Dad. Turn in. I gotta pee."

"Me too. Me too."

"Wha' ... where ... ?" Something that felt like panic seized Henry's gut as he wheeled the Buick to the right. He came close to driving off the pavement. Then the torpor in his mind cleared, a grainy fog sucked out an open window at 70 miles an hour, and when he'd corrected the car's trajectory, he had no more than an instant to register the road sign he was passing. "Rest Stop. Bathroom Faci ..."

"Geesss." Meg jerked erect and grabbed instinctively at the dash. "What's happening?"

"Nothing. Just pulling off. Kids have to pee."

"Good," she said. "Me too."

Henry Craft hadn't been exactly asleep when his children began squealing, but he hadn't been exactly awake either. He'd been driving into the setting sun for close to an hour. His face ached from squinting. In the back, Jeremy and Jane had not made a sound since they'd passed the last town thirty miles earlier. Henry assumed little Jane had drifted off, but he knew Jeremy was awake. He imagined he could actually feel the resentment radiating off his son, onto the back of his neck. The boy could retreat into a lair that allowed no words in or out—a place suited only to fourteen-year-old boys who had failed to persuade their fathers to stop in yet another dusty little town for yet another round of sodas or chips or cheeseburgers.

Meg had slumped against her door with a pillow under her head. Every few seconds, a trembling and uneasy snort came from her gaping mouth. Other than the steady drone of tires on pavement, it was the only sound Henry had heard for a half hour.

The exit led down. The ramp curled around a thicket of cottonwood saplings, their yellow leaves rattling in a chilling breeze, then straightened out into a parking area. The lot was empty, as were the twin cone-shaped structures that served as the restrooms. Teepees. Concrete teepees. A covered walkway connected them. In the center, mounted between two beams painted with grotesque totem pole faces was a single, tin-capped 200-watt bulb over a bulletin board. Henry guessed that there was a map of Idaho on the board. A map, complete with a fat red arrow pointing to this very spot, this rest stop, and a legend: "You Are Here …"

He swung the Buick nose-first into a curb forty yards to the right of the teepees. The headlights exposed a picnic table, planted in the middle of a swath of neglected grass. Beyond that lay another thousand-square-miles of sagebrush, rocky hills, and shadowed hollows, not so different from the thousand square miles they had just crossed—or the thousand square miles before that, all the way back to Cheyenne, where they had spent the previous night.

"Why'd you park so far away? It's freezing out there."

Henry shrugged. "It'll wake you up. Meg. Then maybe you can drive a while."

Once the car was silent, all they could hear was the rustle of cottonwood leaves, so near to falling loose, and all they could see was the reddish outline of the picnic table backed by the silvered shimmer of another thicket of saplings sprouting from a dry washout. Past that, a lumbering grey slope led up to a featureless ridge. In the west, the sky was bleeding from weak orange to an unclean purple.

"So? I thought you guys all had to go."

"Where is everyone?" asked his daughter. "Why isn't anyone else here?"

"I guess no one else needs to pee right now, Jane." Henry tried not to sound patronizing, but with only limited success. His eight year-old clucked her tongue in perfect imitation of her mother.

"Janie's right," said Meg. "I've never been to one of these places when there weren't a few truckers parked around. Or someone."

"The truckers come here to sleep, and it's not even quite night yet. They'll be along, I'm sure. It's too late in the year for vacationers to be traveling through here, the locals would have no reason to stop, and what difference does it make anyway?"

"It's just weird is all I'm saying. We're alone."

"We wouldn't be here either if we'd left after the funeral like I wanted." He paused, waiting to see how Meg would respond. Nothing. Evidently, she was through with that old argument, so he turned to his son. "How about you, Jeremy? You don't need a trucker around to go pee, do you?"

"No, Da-yud. But ... but isn't anyone else coming?"

Henry resisted the temptation to tease his son further, instead opening the door and swinging his feet out slowly. "I don't have to use the bathroom, but I could stretch my legs, that's for sure."

At that, Meg cleared away her pillow, the tote bags, and the trash that had accumulated around her feet. "Come on, Janie," she said. "You and me'll go together."

Were there clouds, Henry would assume there might be snow on the way. It was uncomfortable enough for him to stretch back into the car and feel through the jumble of travel junk for his jacket. Jeremy appeared to be trying to find his hoodie in the back seat, but Henry could tell he didn't want to fall too far behind his mother and sister, already ten yards down the sidewalk. Abandoning his search, the boy crammed his hands into his pockets, hunched his skinny shoulders as high as they would reach to his ears, and shambled awkwardly after them. "Sure you don't have to go too, Dad?" he called back. "We can't be stopping every time you get an urge, you know."

"Nope." Henry grimaced, hearing his own words thrown back at him. *We can't be stopping every time you get an urge, you know* was precisely what he had told Jeremy when the boy had announced thirty miles back that he was "starving to death."

Henry watched after them just long enough to see Jeremy push through the steel door of the "Men" teepee. He set out for the picnic table before Meg and Jane reached the women's. In the pocket of his jacket, his left hand came across a book of matches. He guessed that there was probably a depleted pack of Marlboros in the opposite pocket. This jacket was an afterthought for their trip, thrown into the Buick at the last moment by Meg as a bow to the almighty "what if?" *What if it turns cold while we're there? What if the car gets stuck in a ditch? What if you dirty your sweater?* Before that, he hadn't worn the jacket since late last spring, almost three months before he had quit smoking in August.

He wanted to crumple up the cigarettes immediately and throw their remains into the wind. But now that he once again felt the pack in his hand, the crinkle of cellophane and the soft comfort of the filtered ends, he wanted even more to smoke.

When he reached the table, he took a guilty glance over his shoulder to make certain nobody could see, then pulled one out with his lips. The first match fluttered and died. The second burned on, protected from the numbing wind in his cupped hands. The months-old Marlboro lit up like a desert fire with embers flying off the end.

Just a drag or two. Then no more.

The picnic table was concrete, heavy and solid. Henry propped his butt on it, his back to the restrooms. Should he hear anyone coming, it would be a simple matter to drop the cigarette into the grass and stomp it out before being caught.

That's it, just a drag or two. That's all. I can use it after seven hours of driving.

A big truck rumbled by on the freeway, the noise muffled by the quarter-mile distance and the barrier of cottonwoods, locusts, and scrub junipers that effectively concealed the rest stop from passing traffic.

That's right, I've earned this. Seven hours of driving with no help, I deserve this. I'm not starting up again. A drag or two isn't the same as starting up again.

Maybe it was a trick of tired eyes—a distortion from driving into the setting sun, a visual glitch after a full day behind the wheel—but as Henry carried on his inner conversation, gazing absently into the hills and hollows and spotty sage beyond the perimeter of this meager outcropping of concrete and human presence, he saw something. Or thought he saw something. At first it was no more than a shift in density, up on the featureless ridge of the lumbering slope to the east, past the neglected grass, past the washed-out bottom and the rattling saplings that led his eyes into the distance.

If it was truly there, it was moving. A black, warped figure of questionable substance, standing out against the cold purple sky. Moving against the cold purple sky.

Had this thing—this dubious thing—been climbing the ridge line, or going down the ridge line, it would have crossed Henry's field of vision and might not have been so indistinguishable. Or so unnerving. Either way, up or down, it would have been moving peripherally and away, and he could have shrugged it off. From the side, he might even have seen it was a ranging cow. Maybe an antelope or a deer. Something with four legs.

Something that belonged out there, in the dark.

Yet it—this uncertain thing—appeared to be coming straight forward. Not away from him, but towards. Its size was changing as it came, or so Henry's eyes told him, as though it was climbing up to the ridge from the other side, then over the ridge, then down the near side. His side. Toward the rest stop. This is what his eyes told him. That if it was really there, it had crossed over the ridge and was now growing shorter, disappearing into the dimness that led straight to him.

It's just a cow I'll bet. No man would be out there, not now. Why would a man be out there? A cow, that's what. Maybe a deer. Or a tumbleweed. Could it be a tumbleweed?

He held his breath, staring into the gloom, feeling the wind cut at his back, thinking he might hear something other than wind disturbing the dried leaves in the washout at the bottom of the slope. Hoping he wouldn't.

Did I really even see it? Was something even there? A tumbleweed I'll bet, coming at me like it's something really there.

Then he heard it. Something really there. Something that was not the wind, dragging through the dried leaves.

He didn't know when he dropped the cigarette, but somewhere between the picnic table and the car, he did. It wasn't until he was behind the wheel cranking the key that he remembered his family. "What the hell's taking them so long?" he growled.

The Buick's headlamps once again lit the picnic table and spilled past, reflecting weakly off the low trees, the ashen branches and their restless leaves.

There was nothing.

He waited, letting the closed car and engine purr soothe him. Even as he held tight to the wheel, his hands wanted to tremble. *There's nothing. A tumbleweed blowing over the hills, if even that. What's wrong with you?* He could not imagine ever wanting a cigarette more than he wanted one at that moment.

A tumbleweed? Blowing into the wind?

He backed the Buick away from the curb and let the car idle through those forty yards to the teepees. He steered to a spot directly in front of the tin-capped light bulb and the bulletin board. There, the curb was yellow and "Handicap Parking" had been painted onto the pavement.

The light cover shimmied with a constant, metallic clatter that rose and fell with the wind. Henry had been right about the bulletin board. Pressed under a sheet of Plexiglas was a map of Idaho, the distinctive shape of the state unmistakable even in the quivering yellow light. He could see the fat red arrow he expected to see, even if he couldn't make out what was written on it. He was getting out of the car for a closer look when Jeremy backed out through the steel door that read "Men." He turned to face his father only when it swung shut. "Dad ... ?"

What was it Henry saw in his son's eyes? What was it that curled his fingers into fists and pulled those fists to his breast like insect husks clinging at the underside of something long dead. "Jer? What is it?"

"There's ... there's some ... body in there," the boy stammered. "I think."

He was losing himself in Jeremy's confused eyes. "You think ?" he hissed, knowing exactly what his son meant.

Jeremy's shoulders jerked desperately up and down. "I don't know, Dad. I was in a stall and there was a ... like, I think, a shadow."

"A shadow?" Henry pulled away from Jeremy's fear,

shifting his eyes to the Idaho map and the fat red arrow.

"Yeah. And it moved. That's what I thought. I wasn't sure. But ... I think I saw it move. Then I heard it. I know I did. I heard it. Like something being dragged. But Dad, there's no one in there."

Henry was now close enough to the bulletin board to read what was on the arrow, the red fat arrow, pointing to this exact spot. This empty place in the night where he and his family were. The original legend had been crossed out and a new one had been scribbled in with a thick pen.

"YOU SHOULD NOT BE HERE ..."

Meg came out of the "Women" teepee alone. She called over her shoulder, "Wash your hands when you're done, Hon. I'll be right out here."

She hadn't taken two full steps away from the door before Janie's scream—as much a moan as a scream—came to them. Henry strained to get his legs to move, to carry him toward that urgent terror he could hear in the sound his daughter made, but couldn't. He leaned against a fake totem pole to steady himself.

Meg threw herself back into the door with her shoulder as though she expected it not to open. It did, easily, and through the wedge of open door, Henry could see ... what? A shadow, maybe. A rippling difference on the bathroom ceiling, as though something passed below. A shifting warp in the weak light. Was it? Was it?

Jeremy sighed as though he had no more air to breathe. He'd seen it too.

"Honey? Janie?" Meg held open the door, neither in nor out. Henry watched her shoulders sag. She'd seen it, Henry was sure of it.

Jane was behind the door, but Henry heard her. "Something's in here, Mommy. There is. It touched me."

"Let's get out of here, Dad," Jeremy said, and he was in the car almost before he finished saying it. Janie raced out under her mother's arm and scrambled into the front seat so she could be between her parents. Meg peeked around the door, then knelt down, searching under the stall walls.

"Don't go in there, Mom," whispered Jeremy, far too low for his mother to hear, and Henry nodded.

"That's right. Let's just go."

Meg squeezed in next to her daughter without questioning why the girl was there. Before she'd quite shut the door, Henry was driving away. A mile up the freeway, long after the last spark of feeble light from the rest stop could be seen in the rear-view mirror, Jane was the first to speak. "I didn't wash my hands. Sorry."

Henry started to shrug, but before he could stop, it had turned into a shudder.

POSSESSED
by Bonnie Dodge

My friends like to tease me. "Libby," they say, "you're possessed." They claim I'm in love with a house instead of a man, and it's true. I'm in love with a two-story house I pass every day on my way to work. I have loved that house for years in spite of the rumors, long before I discovered the FOR SALE sign taped to the window. Besides, every man I've ever dated has always been more enamored with his teeth than with me. That's what happens when you work for a dentist.

My friends claim my dream house is an eyesore. Yes, the shutters are sagging. Yes, it needs a new roof and coat of paint. Yes, some think it's ugly. But, when I look at the house, I see what others can't—the way it looked when Miss Johnson moved in with her trunks all the way from Chicago back in 1908, red geranium baskets hanging on the porch and priscilla curtains on the windows.

I've heard the rumors. I know a wealthy banker named Mr. Gibson built the house in 1907 as a wedding present for his bride-to-be. I know he died with an abscessed tooth before the house was completed, and that his fiancé rode the train to Idaho to attend his funeral. The minute his fiancé saw the house, she fell in love. She wrote her mother that she was staying in Twin Falls, and spent the rest of her life waxing the hardwood floors, polishing the windows, and tending her roses. Every morning she would look out the window and say, "Today is bright, white, a perfectly glorious day."

That is, until the day the mail carrier noticed letters accumulating on her doorstep. He knocked. There was no response. He called out, "Hello, Miss Johnson?" She didn't answer. He tried to push the door open, but it wouldn't budge. A week later, the mail was still unclaimed and the postman, now feeling guilty for waiting, reported to his supervisor, who called the police.

They broke through the kitchen door and found Miss Johnson, a shrunken prune lying on the floor in her bedroom, dead. The coroner wrote on her death certificate "cause of death, unknown" instead of "died from natural causes." To settle her estate, the house was sold at auction and the money donated to The Heritage Rose Society. Only the editor from the local paper attended her graveside service where she was buried next to her admirer and fiancé, Mr. Gibson. Some claim she haunts this house even today. They have even seen her peeking behind curtains from her upstairs bedroom window.

Instead of scaring me away, the stories of Miss Johnson and her house intrigue me. Every day I look wistfully at the high, gabled roof and leaded glass, the sunshine on the windows. My dreams are always about the house. The piano sits catty-corner under the window. The maroon sofa is always covered with white lacy pillows. The cuckoo clock in the hallway always calls the hour exactly on time.

Frequently I dream I'm having tea and eating fresh asparagus with Miss Johnson outdoors in her white gazebo. We discuss her roses, the rosemary and thyme growing in the herb garden, the fresh mint we enjoy in our tea. Many mornings I wake, wishing it was still 1908 and I'm on my way to help Miss Johnson clean the kitchen instead of on my way to clean other people's teeth.

So, you can imagine how excited I was when I saw that FOR SALE sign taped to the window of my house. It's a good thing I've always been frugal, that I always walk or ride my bicycle. I never eat out or go to movies. I frequent the library instead of bookstores, and every penny I find on the sidewalk goes into my savings jar. Soon I'll have enough money to make an offer.

This morning the wind is blowing sheets of rain into my face. Teeth chattering, I hurry to work, only to come to a full stop when I reach the corner of Main and Fourth Avenue North where my house has sat forever. The corner is empty. My house is gone. I turn in a circle, rain running down my neck as I hold my umbrella out of the way for a better look. This is Idaho, not Kansas. Houses don't just vanish. But my house is missing, as if someone has taken a giant eraser and removed it from the lot, which is now graded flat, an empty block of dirt transforming quickly into giant puddles of mud.

"What the …?" I rub my eyes and shiver, rain soaking my clothes, my umbrella forgotten.

I'm disappointed, but not defeated. As soon as I get to work I call Robin at the title company. Did someone buy my house? Did she forget to tell me? Instead of eating lunch, I go to the courthouse, but find nothing in the recorder's office to tell me what has happened. For months I search and ask questions, until finally I accept that my house is gone. My heart is broken, my clothes fading into a colorless collection of rags. I don't even want to comb my hair or wash my face. The only part of the day I enjoy is bedtime when I can close my eyes and dream about my house and Miss Johnson.

All winter and spring I mope until one day, south of Filer picking wild asparagus, I look up and can't believe what I see. I have just crossed the railroad tracks, and wham, there my house sits at the end of a dusty lane. I stare in disbelief, grab my bag of asparagus and dash down the lane.

"Libby, slow down." My deceased mother's voice scolds. "You're going to trip on the sagebrush. You're going to fall."

"Am not," I mouth back and keep running.

Even though the house appears to be sitting on a new foundation, the yard is overgrown with weeds. Most of the paint has faded from the outside walls, revealing dull gray wood. Many of the shutters are missing; a few are broken, scattered on the ground. My poor house has never looked so shabby or abandoned.

As I step onto the porch my mother says, "Libby, stop. I don't have a good feeling about this."

"Don't be silly," I say. "This is my house. I'm going inside."

The door doesn't budge. I peer through a window, but the shade is drawn and all I see is my distorted reflection, grinning crookedly back at me.

I soon discover that all the windows on the first floor are locked or nailed shut. The FOR SALE sign that was once taped to the window lies discarded on the porch swing, the red letters faded. Beside it is another faded sign, PRIVATE PROPERTY, KEEP OUT.

"See." My mother picks up the sign and shows me before she settles into the swing. "We need to go before someone shoots us."

I look at my mother. "If you think I'm leaving now, you're crazy." Instead of arguing with her, I search for another way to enter. If I had a hammer or a chisel, I might pry open a door or a window. But all I have is a bag of asparagus.

Circling the house again, I realize to enter I will have to break a window. I pick up a rock, and then put it back down. I can't break the glass. What would Miss Johnson say? She'd probably haunt me forever.

Back on the front porch, I knock on the door and call playfully, "Miss Johnson, are you home?"

"Libby." My mother rises from the porch swing where

she has been waiting impatiently. "Let's go."

I will give the door one last try. If it doesn't open, we will leave. As soon as I get back to Twin, I will start making calls and find out why this house has been abandoned. This time the door opens easily.

"Look, Mom," I say, but don't wait for her. I'm already inside.

Everything is exactly as I have envisioned in my dreams. The piano sits catty-corner under the window, sheet music open, ready to be played. The maroon sofa is covered with white lacy pillows. A picture of Mr. Gibson and his fiancé hangs over the fireplace.

In the kitchen I lift the handle to an old pump and give it a couple of tugs. "Miss Johnson," I say. "Would you like some tea? Maybe some lunch?"

For a building more than a hundred years old, this house is very clean. There is no dust. No cobwebs. No mice. The wood is original; no one has spoiled the walls and ceilings with a cheap coat of paint. The hardwood floors are beautiful. Not a mark or a nail protruding.

Just like in my dreams, there are no bedrooms on the ground floor. I open closet doors and poke my head into the small room under the stairs. I see the doll house from my dreams, a perfect replica of this house still shiny and new. I get excited thinking I might be able to buy the contents, too. Because I'm determined to own this house. This is mine, where I belong.

"Libby?"

I turn at the sound of my name. "What?"

My mother's voice is coming from upstairs, which is odd because I can see her still sitting outside on the swing.

"Did you call me?" I stick my head through the doorway.

"No," she says.

"Do you want to come in?" I hold the door open. "It will soon be time for tea."

She shifts her weight, looks inside, and shivers. "No. And you should get out of there before something happens."

"Scaredy-bones," I tease. "You don't know what you're missing." I leave the door open in case she changes her mind.

Walking around the foyer I can imagine a large Christmas tree at the bottom of the stairs. I will put my grandmother's rocking chair in the corner and hang my creeping Charlie above the window seat in the stairwell.

"Libby?"

I hear the voice again, along with the call from the cuckoo clock. I grab my bag of asparagus and climb the stairs. I will enjoy it later with my tea.

Inside Miss Johnson's bedroom I lay the asparagus on the bed, then go to the window. I move the lacy curtain and peek outside. The sun is shining. The robins are singing.

Today is bright, white, a perfect glorious day.

SHOSHONE INDIAN ICE CAVES: A PLACE OF WONDER AND MYSTERY
by Patricia Santos Marcantonio

In ancient times, the Shoshone Indian Ice Caves were more than rock and ice. Prehistoric Indians called the site "The Cave of Mystery."

A legend tells of a princess of light and fertility named Edahow who was lured by an evil spirit into the cave. She was entrapped in the ice. That's why the Shoshone Indians feared the cave as that evil spirit of darkness, according an account written by the late Russell Robinson who for many years operated the caves sixteen miles north of Shoshone, Idaho, on scenic Highway 75. The legend goes on to say that the ice would someday retreat and Edahow would again bring light and fertility to the Shoshone Nation.

The caves were formed by lava from the now extinct Black Butte volcano more than twenty-thousand years ago. The Shoshone worshiped Black Butte as a fire god. On the east side of the crater rim are six circles of rock called medicine wheels used in spring religious ceremonies, Robinson wrote.

Now a popular tourist attraction, the caves are not only filled with ice, but the history of the area.

Around the 1880s, the caves were found by ten-year-old Alfa Kinsey who lived on a ranch two miles east of them. At that time, ice completely filled the caves. Once discovered, they supplied ice for the town of Shoshone, a hustling railroad stop and jumping off point for mining in Hailey and Bellevue to the north. The ice was cut into blocks and slid up wooden ramps by rope pulleys, and then placed on freight wagons.

The ice was sold to twenty-three saloons and four hotels

on the Main Street in Shoshone, which was the last point of the Oregon Short Line Railroad, said Charles Fred Cheslik, who now operates the attraction with his wife Christine.

Back then, times were wild and wooly. A dirt road wound around the lava flows near the ice caves and was traveled by wagons heavy with gold and silver from the mining towns. Wagons had to slow to ford the Big Wood River, and stories abound of shootouts, holdups and buried gold, Cheslik said.

For sixty-five years, the ice caves have been in the care of the family of Fred Cheslik. While the ice caves have been mentioned as a place of interest on haunted websites, Cheslik said he has never encountered any spirits.

"Maybe they like me," he said with a smile. "So they leave me alone."

But Cheslik does have stories of strange happenings. His uncle Russell Robinson told him a story about working at the end of the cave, which is lit in sections. Only the section in which Russell was standing was illuminated. Russell heard a tap tap tap on the wooden boardwalk that is suspended from the ceiling. He called out a family member's name who he was expecting home from school. There was no answer. Russell then saw the boardwalk sway as if someone was walking over it.

A spirit?

Russell wouldn't say and added that he would deny the story later if asked, Fred Cheslik related.

Cheslik did say his daughter had a pit bull that he described as a sensitive animal. One time in the caves, the pit bull began to growl.

"There was nothing ahead of us, but she kept growling," Cheslik said.

He has taken hundreds of people on tours through the

caves. On one of them was an Indian shaman who claimed there was an evil spirit outside the caves, but a nicer one within.

On another tour a woman asked him, "Are there ghosts down there?"

Fred Cheslik answered, "If there are, I don't know about them."

Whether or not there are ghosts or spirits within, the Shoshone Indian Ice Caves are filled with plenty of legends, wonder and history.

INCIDENT NEAR SUCCOR CREEK
by Maggie Koger

My great-grandmother once wrote how the temperature in their dugout was so cold a spilled pail of water would freeze before she could mop it up. She was familiar with rattlesnakes and rabid coyotes, but also cuddled the bummer lambs her husband brought home. The little woolies bleating could be mistaken for babies crying. They were held tenderly and fed with black rubber nipples stuck on top of bottles. Most grew to a lop-sided adulthood with only three good legs or a twisted neck. These half-cripples were good for a start into the sheep business, or if not, they provided wool, and meat for stew.

When I was a child in the 1950s, I first visited the hillside dugout where my great-grandparents lived near what is now Succor Creek Reservoir in Idaho. My mother told us stories as we bumped along dirt roads in our International Harvester Scout. As I listened, I was already scared because the steep canyon walls loomed over us like giants. And besides, fairy tales and spooky stories seemed more real to me than they may have to my sisters since I was the youngest in the family.

Hazards seemed to strike. Women left at home kept the livestock fed and watered, and cared for the children. They knew their menfolk could be thrown from a horse and suffer a broken neck, or be crushed by a wagon and die before a passerby would find them. But it was children the women worried about the most. A child bitten by a rattlesnake would probably die. Others could be badly burned in campfires, or drowned when flash floods caught them unawares as they waded in the creek.

In such an environment stories of mishaps and weird

events were commonplace. My mother told us about Doña Francesca Rose—otherwise known as Doña Francie—who disappeared one winter night in the 1890s.

Lonely housewives sometimes went months without visitors and years without seeing another woman. In those days, guests were always welcomed because travelers could not find food and shelter easily. Circuit-riding preachers were especially valued and always asked in for a meal and invited to rest up or spend the night in the barn. When preachers were present, all but the youngest children knew to be quiet about Doña Francie. She was a midwife who also brought comfort to women pining for faraway loved ones, fearing the death of a sick child, or wondering how the family could survive another winter.

Doña Francie would also wrap a silk scarf around her head as she sat down with her cards to read fortunes. Although no one really thought she was gifted enough to know the future, whatever she said left them eager to hear her again. Young girls hoped that there might soon be a handsome caller on the way, and young men hoped for a start on their own ranch. Grandmothers liked to hear that their families in the East might visit soon, or that one of the sons working a gold mine would have good luck. Doña Francie's soft voice provided a bit of hope in a perilous time.

Her husband Germany Bill often wore a sombrero to gatherings. The couple was well-known and popular. When a man, wrapped in a blanket with his head almost hidden by his hat and scarf, knocked on Germany Bill's door one winter's night, he was let in. A storm raged, the wind whistled. As he stepped forward snow blew in the door. He gratefully accepted a cup of coffee, but declined further hospitality. Instead, he pleaded for Miz Francie's help. Bill was wracked with a bad chest cold, and although she hated to leave him,

Doña Francie told the man to saddle her horse. She packed her midwife tools along with some food, and they rode off into the night. No trace was ever found of either of them.

Germany Bill searched high and low for months, years even. Rumors floated around. Some claimed a preacher sacrificed himself to become a murderer in order to deliver the families of Southern Idaho from Doña Francie because she was a witch. Others believed that there had been hanky-panky going on between Doña Francie and the mail carrier who disappeared not long after. Folks even whispered there had been no stranger that night. Bill had tired of his wife's notoriety and gotten rid of her himself.

After his wife disappeared, Bill moved to Caldwell where he lost the moniker "Germany" and became a respected city official. In any case, the women sorely missed having a midwife to help with childbirth. Several died while their helpless mates stood watch.

These days ranching has become less common in the region. Many of the old places are now only ruins. Income from traplines dried up long ago and egg money doesn't support a family. So last year when I returned to the site of my great-grandmother's homestead, I expected the quiet emptiness that now fills the canyon walls. I love the fanciful rock formations and the purity of the unspoiled beauty that restores itself when people leave the land alone.

My grandmother was skilled at sketching. Our family cherished her drawings and so it was easy for me to follow the outlines of the horizon to find the gravesites. I stood for a long time in the silence beside the children's graves. Two stillborn girls and two boys who died before their third birthdays rest there. Although no trace remained of the roses she had drawn flowering over the crude headstones, I rejoiced there had once been blossoms to soften the sorrowful spot.

As I remembered stories of my ancestors' struggles to build a life in such a harsh environment, I thought of the happier tales of the harvests and dances in Jordan Valley. Even now I have one of great-grandmother's dresses, some pieces of calico from the homestead curtains, and a couple of raggedy quilt tops that would have kept the living warm and later wrapped the dead. I was consumed with memories and imaginings when I heard a child cry. The sobbing seemed to rise from the earth under my feet and then whirl off — circling high above me. The sound was so real I instinctively reached into my pockets for tissue to wipe away the tears.

The wind calmed as the sun slid closer to the canyon rim. The crying fell to a whisper and faded away. I turned to leave when a sharp reflection of something shiny flashed in my eyes from near the canyon rim. I would never have seen the reflection if I had not stayed to listen to those mournful sounds.

I climbed up and scrambled through shale until I reached a place where erosion had loosened a large rock and left an opening to a small cave. On the ground was an open leather pouch, its contents illuminated by the late sunrays. I reached down and picked up the midwife tools one by one.

I found no Bibles or mail pouches. Instead, I found a couple of badly weathered cards, a rat-gnawed sheepskin, what looked like dry rose petals, and maybe the crooked skeleton of a bummer lamb.

AUNT EDDIE
by Jay Michaels

The thought of ghosts creeps me out. It always has, ever since I was a kid. You might blame my hyperactive imagination. If I saw anything remotely scary as a child, I'd have vivid nightmares. While some of my friends loved horror movies, I always told them to go without me.

Maybe it was because I was terrified of being taken over by an evil force. I'd have nightmares about that, and wake up with my heart racing, yelling for Mom.

When Michael Jackson's "Thriller" music video was released on MTV in 1983, I was a young adult. "The Making of Thriller" behind-the-scenes movie was interesting, but I was still pretty scared by the video.

My friend Bob Rogers and I were working at KEEP-AM/KEZJ-FM Radio while "Thriller" was popular. We listened to the song late one night after we had signed the stations off the air. As soon as Vincent Price's trademark laugh faded into silence, I made a quick trip to the little boys' room. As I opened the door to the hallway, Bob thrust a mop into my face, yelling, "RAWRR!" I was so scared I almost needed to use the restroom again.

Fast forward twenty-five years later, October 2008. A dance troupe at the College of Southern Idaho was performing the familiar dance moves to "Thriller." I was a KMVT-TV reporter covering this anniversary event. I took my camera backstage before the performance, interviewing the dance instructor and some of the students. The makeup artists successfully turned fresh-faced college kids into gory mangled depictions of the undead.

The whiteface makeup made one young lady's dark brown eyes really "pop," and I found myself thinking, "I'm strangely attracted to you … except you look like somebody who's supposed to be *dead*."

Outside the Fine Arts Auditorium, I video recorded the dancers going through their decidedly undead gyrations, went back to the station, and assembled my report for the six o'clock news.

One day a woman approached me at church and said, "I saw the story you did about the Michael Jackson 'Thriller' dance. Was it scary?"

I chuckled, "No. That wasn't too bad. But let me tell you about a time I *was* really scared while doing a news story."

I've covered all kinds of stories in my job as a TV reporter. I've talked to all kinds of people. Occasionally, I have to suspend my personal disbelief in order to tell their story. But I make sure to present that story without any personal commentary. After all, I am a professional.

My assignment editor scheduled me to meet a woman who claimed she was a ghost hunter in a nearby town. I interviewed her and her husband outside their home, and shot video of the still photos that showed orbs and mists, which she claimed were of ghostly origin. With enough information, I headed to the station Jeep to pack my camera and tripod.

As I opened the rear door, the ghost hunter dropped her first unsolicited bomb.

"You have an Aunt Eddie," she volunteered.

I was so taken aback by the woman's comment I scrambled to come up with an answer. Mustering my best reporter's voice, I asked, "Immediate family or extended?"

The ghost hunter pounced. "Extended." She paused. "Eddie is short for Edna."

I mentally ran down the short list of my mom's and

Aunt Eddie

dad's sisters and said as calmly as I could, "No, I don't have an Aunt Edna on either side of my family."

The ghost hunter was undeterred. "She says she's proud of your accomplishments," referring to my nonexistent and noncorporeal Aunt Eddie.

I muttered goodbyes to the woman and her family members — at least the ones I could see.

I shook off my jitters on the drive back to the TV station. Summoning my professional abilities, I wrote a news story about the ghost hunter, and took the script into my supervisor. He read it over, and I told him about my close encounter with "the other side."

"She was just fishing to see if she could get a response," he said.

"I racked my brain trying to remember if I had an Aunt Eddie, or Edna," I replied, "but as far as I know, I don't have one."

I couldn't get rid of the recurringly creepy feeling I had as I edited the ghost hunter's story for the six o'clock news.

So, do I believe in the unexplained? Of course I do. But I'm completely content to keep the paranormal at arm's length. It helps cut down on the creepiness, not to mention the uncontrollable shuddering.

"And *that*," I told the woman at church, "was the scariest story I've ever had to cover for the news."

HAILEY'S RIVER STREET
by Jo Ann Robbins

My office stood on River Street in a quiet brick building. Looking at it now, you'd never know the area was the site of the notorious red light district when Hailey was a bawdy pioneer mining town.

My work required that I spend evenings preparing for educational programs, fairs and the like. I felt safe in the building because Hailey was a genteel and safe community. I usually turned on the lights and locked the door behind me. I checked to make sure there was no one else in the building.

One warm summer evening, I repeated my routine. Working at my desk, I heard a loud thumping sound in the central hall.

"Hello," I yelled, and received no answer. I moved down the hall, checking all the rooms to see if anyone was there. The place was empty. Thinking it merely my imagination or an animal outside, I continued working. I heard the noise again. I looked down the hall and felt a chill. This was not good. I packed up my work, turned off the lights and went home.

As I left the building, the weather was perfect and the moon was bright. The bars and restaurants along Main Street were busy with people enjoying each other's company.

From then on, when I worked at night, I kept the door to the central hall closed. Later that summer, the strange sound happened again. This time I dashed out the door not bothering to check to see if anyone had entered the building. I knew I was alone. Was it my imagination?

I didn't think so.

I didn't mention the noise to anyone because no one else ever worked there at night. Maybe they had similar experiences and knew not to approach the building on warm summer evenings.

Because the thumps sounded so impatient and irritated, I believed it was the madam of the house that once occupied the lot where my office sat. She was conducting business, and I didn't fit into her plans.

Her impatient thumping convinced me that I'd be smart to stay away at night.

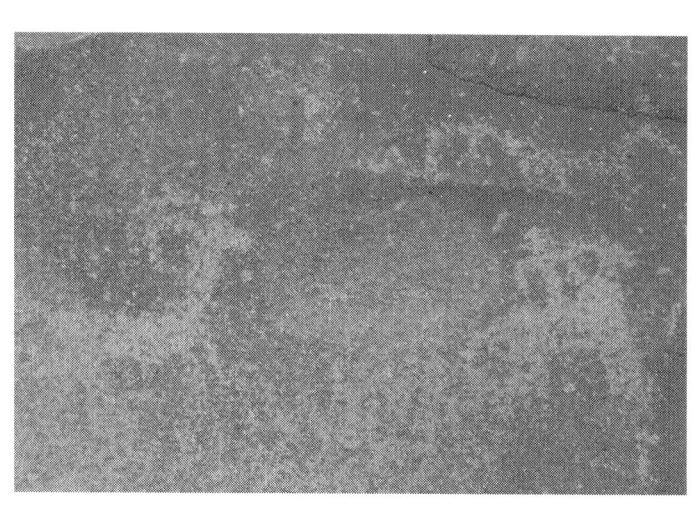

PETROGLYPHS
by Patricia Santos Marcantonio

Petra Littlefoot swears the earth sighed and only she senses its lonely rumblings.

The vastness of desert is both beautiful and desolate. The peaks of the Sawtooth Mountain range to the north are sharp as the teeth of a mythical creature. One ready to devour the unfaithful. On the other side of the mountains are the towns of Sun Valley and Ketchum in a valley of green and wealth. But the land rolling away from that affluence is undeveloped sage and wild grass, which Petra considers far richer.

Although she is only twenty-five, her eyes are older than the land. She sits atop of a worn picnic table where vandals have scratched initials and obscenities. The table is located under an equally worn shelter north of the small town of Shoshone, Idaho, and well away from the state highway. Behind the shelter, a dry riverbed narrows into a canyon that slices into the lava rock and dirt like a cragged wound. A bullet-ridden, old U.S. Bureau of Land Management sign states SPIRIT CANYON.

In the canyon, Petra's ancestors counted the stars and drew pictures of the animals they killed. They danced in the firelight. They left footprints and their spirits behind. She takes a puff of her cigarette and wishes she could read people as well as she does the land.

Sitting next to Petra is Marty Martinez. He is older, bulky, and wears a BLM uniform. Under the brim of his cap, Marty shows hope in his eyes, bright and clear. They both breathe heavy in the one-hundred degree heat. Taking one last drag off her cigarette, Petra flicks it to the ground.

"You're littering." Marty's voice matches his substantial girth.

"It's private property now. They won't mind."

"I still can't figure how you convinced the agency to make the trade with those bloodsuckers," he says.

"The agency got a nice piece of land with a higher value than this parcel. A fair trade."

Marty shakes his head.

"The Wakefield Company plans to develop this into a high-end resort. They promised not to touch the canyon." She wants another cigarette to mask the lie in her mouth.

"There's something more," he answers.

"Don't be so suspicious. Not every developer is the devil."

"Well, they're close relatives." Marty stands and tugs at his belt. His soft face darkens.

Petra has worked with him for six years and has never seen him angry until that day. More than angry. The look is disappointment in her and in himself for trusting her. That makes her lightheaded with shame.

"And just how did this so-called fair trade slip past the environmental and historical groups?" says Marty.

"Way easier than you think. Throw enough lawyers at them and they'll listen to anything."

"Is that supposed to make you feel better?"

She points to the chipped wooden table and bullet-ridden signs. "This place had been forgotten long ago. The canyon land was supposed to be designated a park, but no one came up with the funding. Anthropological resources are at the bottom of the money list. You know that. So the place has slipped back to where it came … into anonymity."

"Cynicism doesn't fit you, Petra."

"How about greed, then?"

"Neither does that. All I can say is your grandfather must be spinning in his grave."

She puts her head down so he cannot see the hurt on her face.

Marty walks a short trail leading to a small area where their trucks are parked.

Petra follows. In the distance, a white Hummer kicks up grey dust on a road leading to them.

"Here they come." Marty opens the door to his truck.

"Aren't you staying for the tour?"

"I just came to tell you goodbye."

"Marty ..."

"I hope they get what they deserve," he says.

"They're rich. Of course, they will."

"And how about you?" Marty asks.

She tries to sound confident, her usual expression that hides what she mostly feels—separateness from everything but the land. "I'll let you know."

"Goodbye, Petra." He gets in the truck and drives away.

"You don't understand," she mutters, then sighs again. That is why she feels more of a relationship with the land and water. People are as distant as the stars, confusing as a cold trail.

The Hummer approaches and parks. John Wakefield emerges. He is fifty and forceful even though out of his element in outdoor clothes, albeit name brands. He wears expensive sunglasses and the nerve of someone who never had to ask twice for anything. Petra would normally hate him and what he symbolizes. Now, he owns her.

At Wakefield's heels is Ben Thompson, younger and clearly subservient. He wears a baseball hat, has a digital camera around his neck, and is clearly miserable in the heat.

"Sorry, Petra. We got lost," Thompson says and then takes a swig from his giant water bottle.

"I figured," she replies.

"This is John Wakefield. Mr. Wakefield, Petra Littlefoot."

Petra extends her hand. Wakefield just nods. She is not surprised at the rebuff.

"Petra knows her stuff, Mr. Wakefield. She was an anthropologist with the BLM until she came to work for us," Thompson says in a hurried manner as if he always lags behind.

"Let's go. I have a dinner meeting this evening." Wakefield looks up at the sky as if he owns that, too.

"Well then, we should get started," Petra says.

Thompson gives a good-natured grumble. "I can't believe this heat. It feels like I'm melting in my shoes."

"It's cooler in the canyon." Lugging her backpack, Petra already is walking toward the entrance.

They start down a rough trail leading into the canyon, treading over polished stones and sandy bottom. Dried moss covers the larger rocks and resembles hair from a water creature. The air smells of dried fish and moisture. Petra smiles. Her feet are sure over the path. She never tires of this place and feels safe here. The world could be destroyed and she never would be harmed within its rocky veins. I am in your hands, Mother, she prays.

The walls of black basalt rise over them as they walk through the canyon, twisting into shiny and mysterious patterns. Rock sculpted by water and time emerge from the river's dry floor like monolithic fingers.

"When the Big Wood River dries during the fall and winter, only then is the canyon revealed. Centuries of erosion created these formations," Petra says. She stops. "But this is what the canyon is best known for—the petroglyphs carved into the walls. Some more than five thousands years old." The carving shows simple figures of men hunting an antelope.

"Nomadic Indian tribes camped here. They believed this place held great magic because it cut into Mother Earth. They recorded their lives on the rock."

Thompson and Wakefield lean closer.

"They weren't much at detail. This one doesn't even look human." Wakefield stares at a petroglyph showing a stick figure with a long neck topped by a circle with radiating lines.

Thompson points to another petroglyph with a figure of a man with large horns. "And what the heck is that?"

"We really don't know for sure. Some of the carvings portray more than mere survival," Petra says.

"Yeah, like what?" Thompson wipes his forehead with a handkerchief.

"Their existence and spirituality. We believe shamans carved some of these drawings while they were in a vision state, as if looking into another reality and recording what they saw."

"Prehistoric graffiti." Wakefield looks at his watch. He doesn't appear to sweat.

"No, Mr. Wakefield, a reminder of the people who once lived here."

"They are kinda cool." Thompson takes several photos. "But they're also really creepy and weird."

"Funny, how this sort of crap is valued, how people want to look back instead of forward. Let's move on." Wakefield turns.

Petra wants to hit Wakefield with a rock. Instead, she leads them farther into the canyon. The walls grow higher over them, as if ready to swallow the intruders. After a short distance, Thompson removes the baseball hat to wipe his shaven head and sips from the water bottle. "Petra, are there snakes here?"

"Probably."

"Rattlers?" His eyes dart about.

"Definitely."

"Thompson, shut up. Your paranoia is a pain in the ass," Wakefield says.

The canyon narrows. The black formations loom more bizarre. Rock sculptures resemble tall angular men with perfect holes in the middle of their bodies. Petra points to a chasm to the right. "Smaller canyons branch off the main one. Stay close."

"Anyone ever die here?" Thompson's voice trembles slightly.

"Not recently. The indigenous people believed if they did die here their spirits would live on in the carvings on the walls."

"That should give you some comfort, Thompson."

"It doesn't," he says.

Petra turns to the men. "In this part of the canyon the petroglyphs become more frequent and elaborate. They're older than time." It is difficult for her to keep admiration out of her voice. She wants to be professional with these people. Wakefield and Thompson study the petroglyphs. Men dance around a fire. Figures hunt or play flutes. Others portray animals and birds. Thompson shoots more photos.

Petra gently touches one of the carved drawings. "I can't blame you for staring. They are so beautiful. My ancestors visited this canyon. It is sacred, part of my blood."

Wakefield ignores her as he attempts to text. "I can't get a signal here."

"... At least to those who believe."

"Thompson, aside from the mining potential of this

Petroglyphs

land, do you see any use for this canyon as an attraction? A profitable one, of course."

Thompson efficiently switches to a business mode. "Probably not, Sir. The liability insurance alone would be daunting. People tripping on rocks, etcetera."

"Then we'll just fill it in."

Petra's mouth dries like the sand floor on which they walk. She is not sure Wakefield is joking. Instinctively, she leans against the canyon wall and spreads her arms out as if to protect them. "You can't do that."

For the first time, Wakefield really looks at her. "Miss Littlefoot, you were well paid to help my company acquire this land. The fact that the government did not know what kind of mineral treasure lay nearby was its fault."

"Yes, that development story was a good one," she says with sarcasm.

"Mr. Wakefield, we might be able to cut away the rock with the petroglyphs and sell them to museums," Thompson says.

"First rate idea."

Petra steps toward Wakefield. "You promised that if I helped obtain the land, you would preserve the canyon and fund research here."

"Haven't you learned that when it comes to money versus promises, money wins out every time? It's the proud history of this country." He smiles.

"These carvings are more valuable than your damn minerals and money. They're more valuable than either of us. You and I will be gone one of these days, but they will still be here."

"How poetic. Your naiveté is charming, but misplaced. You knew what you were doing."

"I'll tell the news media what you are planning."

"It's my land now. They can't stop me."

"There will be an outcry to protect the canyon." She is desperate.

"No one will listen to the person who made this all possible." Wakefield grins with satisfaction.

Thompson isn't listening to them. "Mr. Wakefield, depending on their age, these carvings could also bring in a lot of money from private collectors."

"That will preserve them, Miss Littlefoot. You can help with inventory and authentication. You have expertise in that area, unless you lied."

"I should have known." Her voice is tired. Being betrayed is also in her blood, part of her marrow. Her fingers run along the carved grooves of the petroglyphs. Her stomach swims in bile. What did her people used to do to traitors? Stake them out in the desert? Deny them water and food? Outright kill them? She has no place to go but forward.
Wakefield follows. Thompson lags behind, taking lots of photos—and a wrong turn down a side canyon.

After fifteen minutes, Wakefield's watch beeps. "How much longer?"

"Not far, the canyon becomes too narrow to continue."

Wakefield turns around. "Where the hell is Thompson?"

"I don't know. He stopped to look at the petroglyphs and probably took a wrong turn."

"THOMPSON!" she yells. An echo returns to them. "Let's go back. You've probably seen all you needed since you're going to destroy it anyway."

"With such an attitude, maybe you would like to end your association with us."

"It's not maybe. It's a certainty."

They start back. Petra moves quickly, worried Thompson might have fallen. She slows and freezes in front of a petroglyph. Her eyes widen.

"Why are you stopping?" Wakefield says. He takes off the sunglasses, which dangle from a chain around his neck. In the petroglyph, stick figures hunt animals with spears. They also hunt a man wearing a baseball cap. In the next petroglyph, the man is speared in the back. In the third carving, a spear sticks out of his body.

"Is this your idea of a sick joke?" Wakefield snarls.

Petra's scientific mind calculates the whys and hows. The probabilities and outcomes. But her ancestry opens possibilities with no explanation. And, that fills her with dread.

"Did you think this would force me to change my mind about this place? Well, I don't change my mind."

Her hand reaches out to touch the petroglyphs. Then she withdraws it quickly as if something would touch her back. "I don't know what this is. But I suggest we find Thompson and get the hell out of here." She backtracks their steps.

Wakefield doesn't move. "Not that way."

"It's quickest."

"Find another."

"Up a ways is a side branch that leads out of the canyon. It will mean a little climbing," she says.

"Then move it."

"What about Thompson? He might be hurt. We should look for him."

"We'll send help. Get me out of here," Wakefield says.

She will take Wakefield out and return for Thompson. She knows this canyon. She will find him. "Follow me."

Within minutes, Petra and Wakefield hit the junction where two smaller canyons branch off. They stop and catch their breath from the heat and uneasiness.

"Which way?" Wakefield says.

Petra points to the left. "A straight shot and then out."

He takes off running.

She doesn't stay. She heads back to find Thompson.

Down the smaller canyon, Wakefield weaves around the rocks until he can longer hear Petra calling Thompson's name. As he moves, he thinks, I will fill this canyon in with dirt. Cement would be better but would cost too much. As he runs, the figures in the petroglyphs seem to move with jerky action, like an old kaleidoscope.

"Fill this in," he mumbles. "Wipe it off the face of the damn earth."

The rock figures in the middle of the canyon floor resemble men more than ever. Wakefield feels like he is being watched. He runs on until his irises rise up in shock and pain.

Farther along the main leg of the canyon, Petra calls, "Thompson! Answer me! Wakefield's gone for help. Thompson!"

The canyon is silent.

She spots something on the ground and bends down. Thompson's camera juts out of the sand, rusted. The lens is gone as if the camera had been there for centuries. Slowly, Petra stands. Right in her eyesight is another petroglyph. Ancient figures follow a man with sunglasses dangling around his neck. One of the ghost figures raises a stone ax to the man with glasses. His head split in two. Blood spreads out like a red sun.

Petra covers her mouth to stop from screaming. This is a vision. Her guilt has caused her to imagine these hideous events.

The rock formations close in on her. The harsh shadows hide nothing and everything. Up ahead, the canyon begins to widen. She smiles with relief. The opening is about one-hundred yards away. She counts the distance. Ninety-nine. Ninety-eight. Ninety-seven.

Petroglyphs

Almost there.

Then, her feet refuse to move at the sight of a petroglyph big as a mural. Petra doesn't want to, but steps nearer. "No," she whispers.

Her image is carved there. Behind her stand many figures of men. Figures of the shadow creatures seen by shamans. They carry spears and axes. They are numerous, faceless, malevolent. She is now the hunted.

Petra turns to face what waits for her.

THE HAUNTED FIELD
by Cathy Wilson

The wind howls louder in this rocky field.
Dry barren soil simply will not yield.

Cats won't enter to catch a mouse.
Neither will eagles, pheasant or grouse.

Campers, hikers nor coyotes will come
To this haunted land that sounds a low hum.

The tone is disturbing, vague and unclear.
It must be the dead guardian spreading fear.

The spirit of Farmer Bud dwells here.
Why he remains is not so clear.

What killed the ole geezer is not understood.
Some say it was outlaws, up to no good.

I think his cold heart simply gave out,
While waiting for eyes of potatoes to sprout.

There's one thing that we know for sure.
He guards his land that once was pure.

The Oregon Trail passed by here.
Irrigation arrived and fields grew near.

Potatoes flourished on these lands.
Calluses grew on Farmer Bud's hands.

His sweat and heart dwell in this earth.
He had no time for fun or mirth.

Even in death he protects his fields
As a specter, a shovel and hoe he wields.

Young ones are frightened by his shadowy form.
They stand at the edge and try to stay warm.

Tall tales and falsehoods they spread about Bud.
Boys scoffed at his clothes and boots full of mud.

Unwelcoming, chilling and so full of hate
The field only welcomes its surly old mate.

Bud, the ole coot, is earthbound and sad.
Overworked and lonely, he learned to be mad.

His spirit lingers on in old Idaho.
His foremost thought, "There are taters to sow."

I warn you, don't approach this field of spuds.
The dirt, the weeds, the rocks are all Bud's.

GHOSTS OF THE CANYON
by W. Lenore Mobley

In the Snake River Canyon, sometimes even today, you can hear an echo made by a Chinese boy named Banji Ury. The reverberation of his voice is often so loud rocks fall off the cliff edge and tumble into the river below. Years ago he lived in a one-room house with his mother in the canyon near the river. This is a story of an event in his life that happened more than one hundred years ago.

If heat is the mother of all life, as grandfather said, then water is surely the father, Banji thought. He looked into a clear pool seeing faces that looked back at him. There were times of the day when he saw only fish or his reflection in the eddy along the big Snake River, but early evening was a time when he often saw the faces. He was looking for his half-brother, Jani. When Banji was seven, they played together and he was not lonely. Jani still comes to play like a ghost out of the past. I look for him here, as demons don't have reflections, so Grandfather Ury said.

In the summer months the canyon was baking hot from late morning until night. The heat folded over him like a coverlid and to cool off, he put his feet into the cold river. He was a slight young boy with brown eyes that showed courage when he faced danger. Overhead, the sky was the color of dark slate as the sun set. Banji realized he had been sitting there a long while. He looked up to see a huge round shape that rose black against the canyon walls outlined by the closing of darkness. He recalled the night he was startled by a big man dressed in black who had come upon him. The man had big ears and a small nose, but his mouth looked too wide for his bearded face. He was there to see Banji's mother. The lights went out when the visitor entered the house. That was a signal for Banji to sleep in the shed attached to the back of the house. He usually slept in one of the canoes his grandfather had made before he left them.

Banji remembered his mother did not want to take this house in the canyon, but with little money, the one room dwelling was all they could afford. At times when Banji was asleep he felt the earth tremble. When he woke he knew part of the canyon wall had fallen into the river. The house was a mystery. Often he left the door open and found it closed when no one else was there.

When Grandfather was with them, they had three rooms in a house near the top of the canyon where a stream ran through the yard. Unless they used the boat to cross the river, the trek up the grade to the second level was tiring.

"I liked that place a lot. It was when my half-brother lived with us," Banji said to a frog he had caught along the water's edge. The creature grinned at him—No, surely not, he thought as he quickly released it, and then watched the frog execute a scissor kick with mottled green legs and swim away.

Getting late, the dark corners of the marl were barely visible. What was that—it seemed a curtain was pulled back. But he was used to frightening things happening here. Banji sat there becoming hard as stone against the images flickering through his mind. They were shadows of the night five years ago when he heard a sound coming from the river and sat terrified in his own darkness.

"They have returned," Banji had said, remembering the fleeting, panicked expression on his half-brother's face as he dangled over the side of the boat. That was the last time he saw Jani.

Ghosts of the Canyon

I'm glad I missed the trip to town. The crossing of the river in the darkness always frightened me — even now that I'm twelve, he thought.

She always seemed happy when she returned from town, her face bright as the moon and her skin soft as the clouds. But she looked different that night. She was a kind mother, especially when they were sick.

There were good days when they lived in Grandfather's house and often ate kimchi and colorful rice cakes. "I even liked school there. I wonder, will we ever return to those days?" Banji murmured with sadness.

That night was stark lonely with just him and his mother. The sky was empty and dark, like looking down an endless well. A coyote howled from a distant gully. He shivered from fright and went inside to find his mother already lying on her mat. Banji removed his shirt and quietly lay on his mat beside her.

"Don't fret," she said as she reached for his hand. Her touch made him feel a little better, and he fell asleep.

Many times in the mornings he and his mother worked in their garden. They canned the vegetables that would feed them most of the winter months. In the afternoon Banji invited Jani to go with him to explore all the hiding places among the boulders.

One day of exploring Banji slipped from a ledge when he was climbing and asked Jani to grab his hand to keep him from falling. The fall on the metal was no harder than when he fell onto the boulders the week before. Shaking himself and rising to his knees, he examined what he had fallen upon. An old trunk with a rusty lock.

"Jani, we must break this lock. Gold coins may be inside. I need a rock," Banji sang out excitedly. After several poundings it broke. Holding his breath, Banji opened the trunk lid.

Inside were rusty coins and an old book. Disappointed, he picked the items up and headed back to the house before it got dark.

That night Banji was very upset not finding gold in the trunk. The kerosene lamp hung above him as he lay on his mat and looked through the book he had found. As he turned the pages, a yellowed map of the canyon fell out. Banji saw an "X" on the map. He read a note.

Stand by the big white rock and look north up the canyon where there are two big trees. It lies under a flat stone.

"Say," Banji yelled, thinking Jani could hear him. "I can't wait until daylight. I know of a huge white rock on the second level."

All night the trees near the window were lashed from the wind, and the house again became a frightening place for Banji. Through the dark opening in the window he saw the demon. The same one he had seen after his grandfather left. The demon had matted hair that hung down from its forehead and yellowish eyes that glared, frightening Banji so much he shut his eyes tight. He could hear its low breathing coming toward him.

"Wake up Banji," his mother yelled at him. "You've had another bad dream."

Banji reached for his mother's hand, which helped him relax, but it was a long time before he fell asleep again.

At sunrise, Banji was on his way to the second level of the canyon. He carried a small shovel he used like a cane. He asked Jani to join him on the climb. The trail was easy at first as he went through a wide meadow with tall grass. He stopped to rest. Something slithered through the weeds. A snake perhaps? He had dreamed of a creature, insect-like with reptile features. He quickly moved to the side and jumped upon a large boulder to get out of the grass that hid whatever was coming toward him.

He saw her. They had met before down by the river. The large female coyote snarled at Banji. Her long tail stretched out. The hair on her back stood straight up. Banji was surprised at her response, as she had never been hostile before. She must have her den nearby, so I will let her have space, he thought. The animal let him pass but watched until he went over the ridge.

When he reached the second level, Banji realized the path he needed to follow was soft and lay snug against the canyon wall. Then the earth dropped off. He had to brace himself across the crevices with his feet against the cliff and his back to the boulder. Then he rested and felt for handholds. He edged sideways and carefully climbed over the open space. Roots stuck out for him to clutch. He slid his foot ahead, feeling for footholds. Suddenly, he fell. When he hit the hard surface, his arm crumbled under him. His breath was knocked from his lungs at impact. His eyes were blank.

For an instant, he saw the insect reptile cutting the stone as if it were cheese. The swiftness of its movements baffled him. Dressed in clothes just like his, its eyes protruded like bulging goggles. Banji was whey-faced and trembled at the creature's hissing whisper. He felt the pain from his wrist and saw blood run into his hand. *What should I do next?* Although unsteady, he rose and looked for natural horse balm. He found the tall square-stemmed plant with lavender flowers and minty smell. He tied the moist leaves around his wrist with a piece of tow.

Alone in a strange area of the canyon, he cried out to his ghost half-brother. "Jani, I feel tired. I see blue and white rings around my vision like looking too long into the sun. We must rest." He laid on a large rock. Later, something woke him. Night birds and bats fluttered and squeaked.

"The grove can be as dark as coal. I must move on," he muttered.

"Hello," said the ghost. "Do not be afraid."

"I am not afraid," Banji answered, still lying on the big flat rock. "I'm here," he cried excited. "I found it."

Their new house on the canyon rim was comfortable and close to Banji's new school. His mother no longer had evening visitors, but began to gamble heavily and often paid the Mudang to cast out bad spirits. Banji only visited the old house in the canyon once. Saddened, he found the garden full of weeds. Moving his grandfather's grave to a pretty grassy place near his house, he stopped there often. But he never again went into the canyon or had any more visits from his ghost half-brother Jani.

BILLY
by Bonnie Dodge

I've never encountered a ghost, but I can't say the same for my grandsons. For two summers they hunted ghosts at our farm in southern Idaho. They'd wait until dark , and then form a parade with flashlights as they walked around the yard, shining the lights at the trees or pasture hoping to spot apparitions.

"Can you hear me?" Dante asked.

"Can you tell us your name?" his little brother Kennedy said.

Older brother Dmitri added a "wooooo" or a "booooo" and led them around the yard in circles. When they went to Yellowstone Park with their other grandparents, I sent them off with a list of haunts to investigate while they were there. They had great hunts inspired by Zak Bagins and "Ghost Adventures" on the *Travel Chanel.*

When Dmitri was four, he had an imaginary friend he called Jake. If you bought a toy for Dmitri, you'd better get one for Jake, too. Jake went everywhere Dmitri did. He slept in Dmitri's bed. They even took baths together, splashing and giggling like a tub full of girls. When we took a trip to the Oregon coast, Jake tagged along. We were on our way to see a lighthouse when Dmitri stopped.

"What's wrong?" I asked.

"I'm waiting for Jake. He needs to tie his shoe." In a few minutes Dmitri was ready to go again, jabbering gibberish to Jake. Each step we took to the top of the lighthouse, we had to wait to make sure Jake was still there.

Later, at the end of the day while we were getting ready

for bed, I asked Dmitri, "How did Jake like the lighthouse?"

Dmitri smiled. "He thought it was cool."

It didn't surprise me then, when Dmitri's younger brother Kennedy started playing with Billy. The first time I encountered Billy, he was swimming with Kennedy in the large inflatable swimming pool I erect every summer for the boys. As I watched from the kitchen window, Kennedy waved his hands and jumped up and down. I finished the dishes, dried my hands, and went outside.

"Who are you talking to?" I asked.

"Billy." Kennedy pointed to his imaginary friend.

"Hi Billy," I said, playing along.

"He says 'hi'."

I smiled and said, "How are you today, Billy?"

Kennedy answered. "He says 'he's fine'."

The next day I was setting the table for lunch when Kennedy grabbed another place setting.

"Who's that for?" I counted the plates to make sure I hadn't forgotten someone.

"Billy," Kennedy said. "I asked him to stay for lunch."

And so it went most of summer vacation. Always two peanut butter sandwiches instead of one. Always two glasses of milk. We all grew to expect Billy and wasn't surprised when he spent the nights sleeping with Kennedy in the RV or watching TV in the living room.

One day when Kennedy was helping me weed the garden I asked, "Where does Billy live?"

"Over there in that old barn." Kennedy pointed to the field behind us. I looked, but all I could see were rows and rows of corn. There was no barn, no farmhouse either.

The night before my grandsons were scheduled to return to their home in Oregon, Billy slept outside in the RV one last time. I could hear Kennedy giggling long after his

Billy

brothers were asleep. Oh to be young, I thought as I crawled into my own bed and turned out the light.

The next summer when Kennedy was nine, his father was remarried and Kennedy had a new brother named George. George was two years younger than Kennedy, which made Kennedy happy because he was no longer the baby. While the older boys read books or played *The Legend of Zelda*, Kennedy and George played outdoors riding bikes and ATVs. They'd hunt for cool rocks to toss into the irrigation canal, or spin on the swings.

One afternoon while Kennedy and George splashed in the pool I asked Kennedy if he'd seen Billy.

"No," he said. "He had to go away."

Made perfect sense to me. Now that Kennedy had someone real to play with, he didn't need an imaginary friend any more.

The other day my neighbor stopped by for coffee. We were sitting outside and got to talking about children, grandchildren and imaginary friends.

"I had one when I was little," Joyce said. "Didn't you?"

"No," I answered. "I had two brothers. That was enough." Then I told her about Jake and Billy.

"Billy Carson?" She nibbled on an oatmeal raisin cookie.

"Who?"

"Billy Carson." She finished her cookie and looked me squarely in the eyes. "His folks owned the property next to yours. There was a big red barn where that cornfield is." She pointed and I followed her finger to the same area Kennedy had mentioned the year before.

"Billy had two older brothers who always liked to torment him. One day they locked him in the barn and ran off to play. No one knows how it started, but there was a fire in the barn. When they found Billy he was dead. Papers said he died of smoke inhalation."

"That's awful," I said.

Joyce nodded, and then shook her head as if trying to expel a bad dream. "I thought you knew." She met my gaze and I felt the hair at the back of my neck rise. "Everyone claimed that barn was haunted, so they had a hazing and burnt what was left to the ground."

"What happened to the family?"

"Picked up and left the state years ago. No one's seen or heard a peep from them since."

I stared at the rows of corn. Even though it was a warm summer day, at least eighty degrees in the shade, I'd never felt so cold.

Now, if I hear a tap at the window, or the crunch of gravel in the driveway, or if I see the swings sway when there is no wind, I stop what I'm doing and listen for Billy. Most of the time I don't see anything. But that doesn't mean no one is there.

JUMPING THE GUN
by Conda V. Douglas

I stare at a spot above Lester the Arrester's eyebrows till he frowns and shakes his head. That makes me shake my head, too. I watch to see if he's got it.

"Okay, you can go now," he says to the murderer. He don't got it.

Some days it ain't worth being dead. I watch my latest chance at stopping my hauntin' sashay out the door.

For a man who's supposed to be worried sick about a missing wife, he sure steps lively. I can see the youth in the set of his shoulders. I can see his wife's wealth in the expensive cut of his silk suit.

Sheriff Lester tosses the file on top of a staggering stack.

I want to shout at him. He's called Lester the Arrester 'cause he don't—arrest that is. I don't yell, 'cause he can't hear my ghost voice. Instead, I concentrate on the file folder and shift it in front of him. I doubt he'll take the hint.

I use the breeze from the open window and flip the file open, more for my own curiosity. Yep, as I suspected, the killer's wife is a good decade older than he. Something's familiar about her face, too, like she's an imitation of an old friend. Must be a descendant of the original settlers. Not that there's many of them left, these days.

After the silver ore petered out and the mine closed, a lot of the old timers moved away. I'd been dead a good ninety years. Good old Starke turned into pretty much of a ghost town for decades, haunted by a few lost souls with no other place to go.

And me, the town's one ghost.

Those were lonely years, just sitting around watching people grow old and die. No chance for me to catch a murderer and quit haunting. Worried me plenty, too. Figured I'd never get out of town.

Times change. Starke is Idaho's newfangled ski resort—fool idea if you ask me, which nobody did. Every day some rich idiot shows up wanting to break their necks on our mined-out mountain. Like that young fancy man who just strutted out of here.

Lester stares at the file and taps his finger on the page, on the woman's age. Maybe he's taking my hint. He moves his finger to the woman's maiden name and frowns. I don't keep up on the residents like I used to, but I know her maiden name belongs to an old ranching family. Land values sure have jumped in the past ten years.

Lester shakes his head and puts the file back.

I think about materializing and giving him a piece of my mind. He's letting a murderer walk away, and seeing a ghost dressed in cowboy boots and six-guns might wake him up to that fact. Trouble is, after I materialize I always end up with a walloping headache and a powerful thirst for whiskey. Ain't hardly worth it.

Lester turns back to his computer where he's running a check on a drug smuggler. I look at the pile and feel a bit mean spirited, even for a spirit. I never had such a workload. Crime sure has gained popularity in the past hundred years.

'Course we had high rollers in the old days, too. They thought they were above the law, least for a while. After I'd strung 'em up they were above the law, at least in body. Simpler in those days, none of this silly "forensic" stuff confusing the issue, and, God take me, computers. Just me in the old days, Starke's law and order all rolled up in one man.

A portrait that's supposed to be me hangs behind

Lester's head. Always bothered me that it's of the town's undertaker, and he looked a great deal more like a sheriff than I ever did. I sure didn't have that full head of hair. Though after a hundred years, I have a hard time remembering my looks. Still, an honor.

I like to think it's because of my one-hundred-percent conviction record that I'm remembered. In my career of six months, I caught horse thieves, claim jumpers, rowdy drunks, and hung two murderers. Found out later neither of 'em were guilty. Now I've got to catch a real murderer before I can quit haunting.

And here one sauntered out after leaving a missing person's report. He figures he's taking the suspicion off himself. I expect that's for when the body shows up later, so's he can inherit her money. Hang the husband, I always say.

The phone rings. Lester answers, a big frown on his hairless face. Never did figure out why any lawman would be clean-shaven and baby smooth—just gives the wrong impression. Lester grabs his coat and runs out the door.

I don't think he's headed for our friend's house. Probably another cocaine bust. Meanwhile, our murderer is home free. Or is he?

I stare at my portrait. Yep, my centennial. It's getting old being an old ghost. I decide to do something about ending my haunting.

I'm not supposed to catch this guy by myself, just lead the living sheriff to it. What harm would what they call a "stakeout" do? Besides, I'm the best person I know for the job. I can't be spotted unless I materialize.

I sorta think myself over to the address on the file form, sure beats walking. I used to catch rides on carriages, but I've never liked riding around in those automobile death boxes.

The address is an ugly mansion that looks like it's been

thrown together out of discarded mining shafts. Must have cost the wife plenty. A couple of sport car monsters, one red and one black, are parked out front. From the girl mess in the red one, it's hers. So where'd she run off to without her car? There's no taxi service in little old Starke. I wish Lester was here to wonder the same thing. Since he's not, I float up the walk and in through the front door. The inside foyer is as ugly and expensive as the outside. Money makes murder.

A shovel is propped up next to the door. Sloppy. Where did he bury her? In the cellar?

That's where we found old Mrs. Murgutroud. Hung her widower the same day. Some said I shouldn't have been so fast to hang a man over eighty. Quick justice, I called it. I found out later that he'd buried her there to avoid paying for a funeral. Too cheap to live, I figure, served the old boy right.

The husband comes down the stairs, forcing me back into this crazy present. He sure don't look like the worried sick fellow what left the office. He's changed into fancy jeans and a pink silk shirt. That shirt alone might get him strung up in my time.

The guy's name is Jody Farragut. What kind of a name is that? No wonder he's turned out bad.

He's whistling. If Lester could hear that. Jody carries a leather suitcase, and it's heavy by the way he's using both arms. Wonder what's inside? Where's he headed?

The doorbell interrupts him. He frowns, and I think he's not going to answer. Then it rings again like somebody's froze their finger to the button. Quick, he puts the case out of sight and shovel, too. He opens the door to another reason for murder.

She's young and got a great figure, almost all of which I can see. She's wearing a skimpy handkerchief of a top and shorts so short they might as well not exist at all. Some things have improved in this century, although I find it real difficult to concentrate now. When alive, I used to get excited at a glimpse of ankle.

"Hey, baby," she says, slipping inside like a water snake racing down the creek.

"What are you doing here?"

"Seeing you." She gives him a syrup smile.

He don't smile back. "I told you not to come around here yet." He looks past her, out the door.

"Don't be silly, nobody's seen me." She slips her arms around his neck and snuggles all that glorious flesh against him. It's enough to make me wish I had a body again.

"You know what this podunk place is like." He doesn't embrace her back. "Blink at another woman when you're married and it's all over town."

"Ah, lover, I just couldn't stay away." She punctuates her protest with a kiss.

He doesn't kiss back. Cold-blooded murderer, sure enough. He pushes her away.

She pouts. "You got the money?"

"No, not yet," he says.

"The tickets?" Her eyes shine with greed.

"When would I have time to get those?" He's angry now, and she cringes away from him. I'll bet he's a woman hitter. Didn't use to hang men for that. Should have.

"But what if they find her?" she asks, real soft and quiet.

I lean closer. I'd sure like to know where he put the body.

"They won't find her." Jody looks toward where he hid the shovel.

"Why not?" she says. "Where'd you hide her?"

"Shut up." He grabs her arm, lifting her to her toes. She

screams. Maybe I'm about to witness another murder.

He half pushes, half carries her to the door saying, "I'll call you when I'm ready. Until then, don't come here." He ends this with a hard shove out the door.

She stumbles and falls on the steps, and before he slams the door I see her face. If there was any love between these two, it's gone now.

He smirks at the door, fetches the suitcase and opens it. I see an aeroplane ticket on top of stacks of money. Only one ticket. He's ditching the girlfriend.

I know I have got the measure of my man, now. Sleeping around, wife catches him, wants a divorce so he kills her. Now he's lost what little nerve he had and he's bolting. If I was still sheriff, he'd be kicking air by now.

Jody glances at his watch, frowns, and races up the stairs. Got to catch his way out of town. I follow him to the top of the stairs and hover there. I don't know where Lester is, and this fool's escaping. If I don't do something quick, I'm going to be haunting for another hundred years. I get an idea.

I wait till he comes out of the bedroom, dressed in a suit. As he reaches the first stair, I materialize right in front of him.

"You're under arrest," I shout.

I forget he can't hear me. The front door opens. Must be the girlfriend, back for another round.

He's startled. His foot misses the first step and down he tumbles. Good. A couple of broken bones will keep him occupied until Lester arrives.

Only it's not the girlfriend screaming at the bottom of the stairs, it's his wife, and Lester is with her. My murder suspect's broken a bone all right, a neck bone, from the way he's laying all twisted.

After a couple of minutes, Jody's ghost joins me, and

we both stare at his corpse. Lester's called the ambulance and then gone to get the wife a drink. I sure could use one, too.

"I thought you killed her," I say to him. I'm real disappointed.

He stares at his body, stunned, or like he's figuring a way to get back inside.

"Forget it, you're as dead as I am," I say. "How come your wife ain't dead, too?"

He looks at me, then back to his wife, who, now that Lester's gone out of the room, is smiling.

"I was going to kill her, you old fool," Jody says.

"Going to?" Now I'm feeling real confused. Same feeling I used to get often when I was alive. Sheriffing ain't easy work.

"She was coming into Boise this afternoon on a flight from San Francisco. Went shopping, you know? I was going to pick her up at the airport, kill her, bury her, and then head to Mexico. She must have caught the puddle jumper to Starke to surprise me."

"You wanted a divorce?"

"No. Had a prenup, I wouldn't get a dime. I couldn't stand another day being married to the old bat."

"But the money?" I'm trying to take all this crazy fool nonsense into my old ghost brain.

"We got a joint account that I emptied this morning. What do you think I was going to live on in Mexico? Dust?"

Reminds me of the second murderer I hanged. Found a fellow with a satchel full of money in a seedy hotel one day. I could see his poverty in the sorrowful droop of his ancient shiny suit. His lady friend, the only clerk at our bank, had gone missing. So I figured I had me a murderer with embezzled funds, and since it was the weekend we had a Sunday hanging. Turned out on Monday he'd come into quick money by gambling on Friday night, and sent his lady friend shopping for her wedding dress down at the state capital Boise.

When the bank clerk got back, she was none too pleased, seeing as how she'd never see thirty again, and he'd been her only way out of spinsterhood. Fact is, the whole prospect of spending her life as an old maid so depressed her she used her lover's gun to shoot me. Hope it cheered her up some. They didn't hang her for her crime; the jury seemed to believe she had just cause. Put her in jail, where she married the matron's brother. It turned out all right for her. But I'm still dead, and a ghost to boot.

Jody had every intention of killing his wife. Now that he's a ghost, he's got to save somebody from being a murderer.

Seems to me, we're in competition one with another. I've got to catch somebody after they do murder, not before. My fault for always jumping the gun, I guess. Jody's plenty upset about being dead.

But at least now, I've got me some company.

THE HAUNTING OF ROOM 10
Soloaga house in Shoshone, Idaho
by Karma Metzler Fitzgerald

Room 10 doesn't look scary. It's square. White walls. Curtains sporting a geometric design hang in the solitary window. There's an old bed to the side. Other than that, the room is empty.

Maybe.

When Jann Thomsen bought her three-story home in downtown Shoshone, the real estate agent who had lived in the house told her it was haunted by nuns. She paid little attention. "I thought he made that part up."

Their first night in the house, her boys slept with her. They were both more than old enough to sleep on their own, but after hearing the stories, they were afraid. That night Jann had a dream. Catholic nuns came to her.

"The nuns told me we were welcome. No harm would come to us." From that moment on, she didn't worry. The ghosts of a young woman and a forty-something man of short stature appear every so often. He's protective of Jann, who believes he is the occasional resident in Room 10.

From time to time, visitors stop by the house wanting a tour of the historical building.

"One man told me he'd stayed in Room 8 and the bed had levitated off the floor — while he was in it."

Jann redecorated and restored the main floor, which served originally as a boarding house predominantly for Basque sheepherders. She has redecorated some of the rooms upstairs, each with its own motif. The ghosts let her know if they disapprove of anything. "If we are working on something they don't like, the room will get very cold or something weird will happen."

They also make their presence known if they don't like Jann's guests. One night, after she had hosted a male visitor, the man from Room 10 came to her in a dream and told her to "'stay away" from him. Turns out the ghost was right. Her guest was not as nice as she initially thought. "Listen to your ghosts," Jann said.

Over the nineteen years Jann has owned the home, she has occasionally taken in boarders. One boarder was in the shower upstairs when a thin woman with long, dark hair interrupted, and told her to "get out." No other woman was in the house at the time. The boarder, a Native American, performed a "cleansing ceremony," but nothing changed.

Jann believes the female presence may be the spirit of the woman in a portrait that hangs at the bottom of the stairs. The painting came with the house, and she never saw fit to move it.

The portrait may be of a relative of the original owners of the house, Domingo and Antonia Soloaga, who immigrated to Shoshone from the Basque Country in Spain. Like many Basque families, they set up the boarding house to provide a home to the hundreds of Basque sheepherders who came to the Magic Valley to work. In the summer while the herders were on the range, the rooms were rented to their wives and children or to other area workers.

The large yard used to be all garden with garlic hanging in the sheds and an abundance of plots to grow food. The herders returned in fall after the sheep had been brought in from summer range. Jann said she notices more peculiar things going on in the autumn, which would have been a busy time at the boarding house. In particular, her protector in Room 10 is most active then. People who have stayed in Room 10 report he sits in the corner. She has no idea who the man might be.

Jack Soloaga didn't either. His grandmother Antonia made it clear that under no circumstances was he ever allowed to go near that room. "Something tragic happened there," he said.

Jack has wonderful memories of running through the halls with his cousins — but only on the main floor. The second floor always made him uncomfortable, and the basement was downright creepy. "She (Grandma Antonia) would send me down there for groceries. Doors would slam. There were always shadows. Someone would touch you." When he'd tell his grandmother of the unusual events, she'd believe him, "but she'd laugh and laugh."

Jack experienced all sorts of odd things while staying at the house. For example, the room he slept in had French doors. Even though he would carefully lock them each night, they would be wide open the next morning. Jack has no explanation for the strange happenings or ghosts. He said the nuns would make sense because the Soloagas are devout Catholics. Over the years, a number of people died in the house, but he didn't know why any of them might linger.

As long as he was near his grandmother, he never felt truly threatened. She had her own powers. She'd rub garlic on warts, say something over them and cover with a bandage. The next morning they'd be gone. "I don't know how she did it, but it worked every time."

Jack and Jann are friends. He will occasionally bring people over to the house for tours. His kids say they want to spend the night in Room 10. Jack has only one thing to say about that. "You are crazy."

THE WINNEBAGO PHANTOM
by Sherri George

My husband Mike can't resist a deal. Craigslist, yard sales, cars with hand-lettered "For Sale" signs in their windows, call to him like sirens to Ulysses. So when a disreputable Winnebago motor home rumbled into our driveway one Saturday afternoon, I felt no surprise.

"Where did you get that?"

"A guy in Buhl had it in his driveway," he shouted out of the driver's side window.

"And how much did you pay?"

"A thousand bucks. The engine alone is worth that. And it runs."

It ran all right, with gouts of blue smoke pouring from the tail pipe. "You better shut it off," I said.

"Not until we decide where to park it. The guy had to jump the battery."

At last the mighty ark came to rest in our side yard. Chug chug putt, the engine coughed and died. Mike poked his head out the door. "This will be great. Half the work is done already."

I looked in. Half the work had indeed been done— the ripping away of interior. Shreds of harvest gold carpet remained on the floor. A copper brown table poked up from the ruins of a banquette. Peach and seafoam green wallpaper, a forlorn refugee from the '90s, peeled away from the dark paneled walls. "Great project vehicle," I said. "What year is it?"

"From 1973." He lifted a carpet-covered box between the driver and passenger seats to reveal an engine worthy of a semi. "Look at that. They don't make 'em like this anymore."

"Well, of course not. Gas was, what, a quarter a gallon?"

"More like fifty cents. This has a forty-five gallon tank."

I did the math. In 1973, twenty bucks would have nearly filled the thing. Now $150 might come close. "We can fix it up, but we can't afford to drive it anywhere. I guess we can use it for a retirement home."

He laughed. "Aw, c'mon, it'll be fun. Who ever dreamed we'd own a Winnebago?"

I figured this monster would keep him busy for several weeks and out of yard sales from Buhl to Burley. "All right, but we're getting rid of the '70s colors. I'm having disco fever flashbacks."

I went out the next day to clean the beast up a little. Dust coated the puffy brown vinyl dashboard. Behind a cracked plastic panel I found a rectangular opening for an eight-track player. Grateful for MP3s, I thought it would be fun to hear the grinding and the shift between tracks again. I looked under the dash, where cut wires dangled from the back of the player. I punched the "play" button for old times' sake. "On the south side of Chicago," sang Jim Croce from the speakers.

Wait. Impossible.

There was no juice to the eight-track player. But here came some of the top hits from my freshman year of high school. I must have hit the radio button. While dusting I listened to Helen Reddy, Anne Murray, and Karen Carpenter's "It's yesterday once more." But no announcer. Then ... Grind. Click. The tracks shifted.

"... you used to say live and let live ..."

A shiver snaked down my spine and the afternoon turned cold. Time to go in and find something for supper.

Over hamburgers and salad, I asked Mike, "Did

you notice anything funny about that eight-track in the Winnebago?"

"Nothing except that it's hammered. Guess I'll put in a CD changer."

"Is it hooked to the radio somehow?"

"Nah. Looks like there was a CB radio, too. Bet that eight-track hasn't worked for years."

Except it had. That afternoon. The shiver prickled along my back again.

I gathered my courage the next weekend and went out to the Winnebago. Mike perched on our rickety stepladder, waxing the aluminum exterior, taking extra care on the "W" logo. "The paint is in great shape," he said. "I bet he was garaged for a long time."

"He?"

"I decided on a name. Clyde."

"How did you come up with that?"

"I don't know. It just fits."

"Clyde. Hmmm. Hope there won't be a Bonnie to match." I clambered up the step into the interior. Mike had started stripping the wallpaper, so I finished peeling jagged pieces. It wouldn't be so bad after all. Turquoise paint over the paneling and Hawaiian print curtains. A nice summery island vibe instead of autumn gold and brown worthy of "That '70s Show." I imagined Ashton Kutcher perched in the driver's seat wearing a polyester shirt and a look of brainless bemusement.

I stepped to the galley at the rear of the motor home, past the copper-colored refrigerator and gas range, and looked out the back window. Time for Windex and paper towels — everything looked foggy. And the trees ... smaller. Much smaller. Saplings.

I shook my head. Dirty glass, nothing more.

And then an aroma, a whiff of prom night in the back

seat of a '62 Impala, the perfume counter at Sprouse-Reitz, Roger Moore as James Bond igniting a can of deodorant with a cigar.

Brut.

I cranked the louvered window open and stuck my nose against the screen. Mmm, nothing like that dusty metallic smell. But when I turned back to the galley, the prom-night-perfume-counter fragrance assailed me again.

Mike leaped in through the door. "Honey, did you get into my wallet? I swear there was a twenty in there, and now it's empty. Hey, thanks for finishing that wallpaper. I'll start sanding the paneling when I have time."

"No, I didn't take any money. Do you smell something in here?"

He took a deep breath. "Plastic."

"Nothing ... aftershavish?"

"Smells like an old trailer to me."

I leaned against the galley counter. "I smell Brut."

Mike laughed. "Hey, maybe I can get one of those pine tree air fresheners and douse it with Brut. It'd be just like the 70s."

Too much like the 70s. Like I could go in, turn on the console TV and adjust the rabbit ears to see Gerald Ford's earnest square face on the screen. Like I could go to McDonald's, get a two-hamburger meal with fries and a drink, pay with a buck, and get change back. Like a fellow in a Qiana shirt unbuttoned to his navel stood in this tiny kitchen with me, so close I could smell the Binaca on his breath. *Hey Foxy, what's shakin'?*

My knees, that's what.

The Winnebago Phantom

Over the next few weeks, no more aromas or 70s hits emanated from the Winnebago. I quit looking for clackers and mood rings stuffed in the cubbyholes, or a leisure suit hanging in the closet. Mike found a large scrap of taupe Berber on Freecycle and installed it. He rebuilt the banquette and foldout sofa bed, and I added turquoise and cream cushions. The sanded paneling took its coats of "Caribbean Dream" paint without protest. I sewed surfer-print curtains. My 1973 nightmare became a 2011 island sanctuary.

The night after I had installed the final set of curtains, stiff with spray starch, I looked out into the driveway before I went to bed. The Winnebago's windows glowed soft gold. Strange, Mike was usually careful to turn the lights off before he came in for the night. I threw on a robe and slippers and padded out.

As soon as I opened the door, the lights went out. I flipped the switch by the door, but nothing happened. All dark inside, smelling of fresh paint and starched fabric. And—Brut? Not again. Not my Qiana-clad phantom. "Stop it," I said, "just stop it."

Catch you on the flip side, Foxy.

Back in the house, I crawled into bed and stuck my icy feet against Mike.

"Hey, what was that for?" He gave me a playful kick.

"For bringing home that Winnebago and whatever lives in it."

"You're trippin'," he muttered.

"Good night, John-Boy," I answered.

My parents came for dinner that Sunday. I couldn't wait to show off our motor home. I opened the door and gave my mother a hand up the steps.

"Oh my," she said. "Wonderful job. You didn't tell me you were going to restore it. Where did you get this carpet?"

"In town." I stepped up. But wait, that wasn't Mike's taupe Berber. My feet sank into pristine harvest gold shag. Burnished dark paneling covered the walls. The banquette and bed sported avocado and brown striped cushions, and owl-print curtains covered the windows.

"This is so *cute*," Mom said.

You're sick, Michael, sick, I thought. Why would he do this to me? He'd played practical jokes before but this was too much.

"If I could put time in a bottle," sang Jim Croce from the speakers.

"It takes me back thirty years," Mom said. "Too bad they don't have shows for motor homes like they do for cars. You kids would win first place. And where did you find a Brut air freshener?"

Mike pulled himself in through the door. "Holy crap."

"Why did you do this?" I hissed.

He stared, mouth agape. "It wasn't me."

Mom beamed on her way out. "Lovely, lovely job. I'll see if I have any needlepoint pillows in the basement for that sofa. Your father is going to absolutely adore this."

Mike and I avoided looking at each other for the rest of the day. After Mom and Dad had waved goodbye and the dishes were done and put away, I gazed at the silent Winnebago, the "W" logo stark in the moonlight. Then the windows glowed with that same golden radiance. And the music. The distinctive, driving beat that had taken me through high school and into college. Did I see a shadow moving back and forth across the windows?

I was furious. Whoever it was, whatever it was, this was *our* property. I wished briefly for a gun, then went to the buffet and grabbed the bottle of Lourdes water my Catholic grandmother brought back from her pilgrimage. Mess with

The Winnebago Phantom

me, will you, phantom of the Winnebago? Remember that hit movie from the 70s? *The Exorcist?*

I strode to the driveway, flung open the door of the motor home, and jumped up the steps. Aftershave, the strongest I had ever smelled. "Your mama don't dance and your daddy don't rock and roll," sang Loggins and Messina. And there in the galley, stood the phantom.

Silky Qiana shirt, with an abstract print resembling targets, unbuttoned to show the hairy chest and the gold chains. Brown polyester bell-bottoms held up with a wide leather belt. Hair in a white-guy 'Fro, sideburns and mustache. He stared at me. "Foxy?"

"Clyde?"

"How do you know my name?" He started toward me.

I held up the bottle. "I have holy water, and I'm not afraid to use it."

He stopped. "Hey, Baby. Mellow out."

"What did you do to my walls? My curtains?"

He shrugged. "I don't know. It just happens. I take the old girl on the road whenever I can, when the moon is right, put in an eight-track and keep on truckin'. She goes back to the way she used to be. Runs better since you folks have been working on her."

"You mean you drive our motor home … back in time?"

"Guess you can say that. But hey, I always gas her up if I've got money."

"Where does a ghost get money?" I couldn't stand on my trembling knees anymore and collapsed on the avocado and brown sofa.

"Your old man left his wallet in here one day."

I squinted toward the dash panel. Sure enough, the needle I had never seen above E now hovered just below the F. "You can take money … back to the 70s … and fill up the gas tank?"

"For sure." He sat on the other side of the sofa. Not quite solid, not quite there. "Bonkers, ain't it?"

Mike appeared at the door. "Honey, what are you doing out—hey, who are you?"

The phantom squinted at him. "Original owner, you jive turkey."

"Mike," I said, "this is Clyde. From 1973. And he can gas up the motor home for twenty dollars."

Mike stood for a long moment, looking from me to Clyde and then around the interior. "You used to say, live and let live," crooned Paul McCartney and Wings from the speakers.

"Clyde," Mike murmured. "Talk to me, man. Let's work out a deal."

I squinted. The décor wasn't so bad, really. I could get used to it. I might even learn to like it.

Now Mike and I drive the Winnebago around southern Idaho, and even farther afield, when the moon is right. People in RV parks knock at the door and beg to see our authentic restoration. When they ask where we got the supplies, we smile and refer to our confidential source. Before we pull out the bed and settle down between Hollie Hobbie sheets, a sure sign that even phantoms have a sense of humor, we leave a twenty-dollar bill on the driver's seat. And sometimes I wake to the sound of rolling wheels, the aroma of Brut, the grind and click of the eight-track, and a puffy-haired phantom truckin' through the night.

10-4.

NIGHTHAWKS
by Grove Koger

"It was my uncle's voice, but ..."
She had repeated the words several times, never finishing, but they waited patiently. Some of the story — well, some of the backstory — they had pieced together over the years. They shared an extensive common history, the group did. Full of bravado, they called themselves the Nighthawks, after the famous Edward Hopper painting. They had grown up together, gotten drunk together, loved together, but then there were the bits and pieces that came trailing along, the beforehand bits. One of them involved Laura's misadventure in the Owyhee Desert when she was little. A misadventure for her, and really bad business for her uncle. He had left the family party to look for the young lost Laura, never to return. But she did, wandering back a while later clutching the lizard she had been chasing.

She blamed herself a little, couldn't help it. Who wouldn't? Yet the uncle was an experienced hunter and hiker, if not quite a mountain man. It was bizarre. The search parties — there were a lot of those — eventually wore themselves out, concluding he had fallen down a crevasse. There were a lot of those too.

Laura returned, by herself, every year to the scene of the, well, *event*. Every anniversary. Okay. But this year had been different.

"It was my uncle's voice ..."

The Nighthawks waited, watching her carefully. The fire crackled.

"It was my uncle's voice, but his face ..." She screamed. They jumped up to hold her. She was shaking, couldn't stop.

But then she pushed them all away, sat back down, scooted closer to the fireplace and told her story.

☙ ☙ ☙

As usual, Laura drove into the mountains. She knew the place well, just over the rise by the creek. This routine helped keep the experience at bay for the rest of the year. This time she was a little late. The shadows stretched out over the hummocks and down the gullies, and a cold breeze had sprung up, but that didn't matter, did it? She never stayed long, just hiked around a bit, sat for a time on one boulder or another, and stared at the creek.

She didn't expect anything, but knew she had to complete the routine and then drive back and meet up with the Nighthawks for the rest of the evening. She was alone, but she was tough and smart—always kept a little canister of pepper spray on her key chain. Twirling the chain around her index finger and watching a solitary bird sail across the sky, she heard someone calling her name, stretching it out into long syllables.

"Lau-ra. Lau-uu-ra." Kept calling. "Lau-uu-ra." The voice was familiar.

To make a long story short, and she desperately wanted to do that, the figure of a man appeared over the top of the rise on the other side of the creek, striding along, looking this way and that, calling. For an instant she thought it might have been one of the other Nighthawks, the only people who would have known she was right there, right then. But no, of course not, the voice was wrong, wasn't it? Plus, he was approaching from the wrong direction where there was no place to park, just a hundred miles of desert. But there he was, striding toward her and calling.

"Lau-uu-ra."

Just as she recognized the voice, the sun, low in the sky,

broke through the clouds and shone on the man's face.

🦇 🦇 🦇

"It was *him*, looking for me." She screamed, remembering the face, and the Nighthawks held her. "But his face ..." She took a breath. "This is the strangest thing that's ever happened to me. Things like this don't happen to *anybody*, not really. God, I must have driven here like a *sonofabitch*. Give me another beer, *please*." She drank.

"Okay, I'll say it. It was my uncle. Looking for me, the way he must have been looking for me twenty years ago. It can't be, but it is. Was. I don't know what to do." She drank again. "I don't know what to do. I have to be careful or I'm going to be sick."

She took a deep breath, did indeed feel more than a little sick. "It might help to be sick, might be just what the doctor ordered, ha ha." She turned in her chair. Starting to get up, she felt self-conscious. But at the same time knew that she had never loved them so much, the Nighthawks, all of them together, loved them all. They'd help get this straight, whatever it was, help her understand. She started to smile, looked up at the faces she loved, and ...

"No, NO, NO! NOT YOU TOO! NOT YOU TOO! WHAT'S GOING ..."

She tried to break free, but they were holding her again, not tightly, just holding her, holding her up, as if she'd understand if they held her long enough, but she wouldn't, she wouldn't, she wouldn't, not ever.

SPIRITS OF THE OLD STATE PEN
Old Idaho Penitentiary, Boise
by Patricia Santos Marcantonio

Within the thick sandstone walls. Under the harsh turrets. Behind the rusted bars. In the confining cells. The Old Idaho Penitentiary still echoes of punishment. But those echoes may be more than history.

Visitors and staff have experienced the unexplained, says Amber Beierle, Idaho State Historical Society Education Specialist/Visitor Services Manager at the Old Penitentiary.

"We must always lock the door to the Gallows room as it is only opened for guided tour programs and special events. Several volunteers and staff members have reported locking the door, only to come back later to find it wide open," she says.

Throughout the prison, visitors have claimed to hear voices, have a strange feeling of uneasiness or "heaviness," or have been physically touched by a "presence." One visitor said she felt someone reach out from a cell and say "pretty" as she walked by. Many of these paranormal incidents have taken place in "Siberia," the name given to solitary confinement, and 5 House/Maximum Security, where the gallows and Death Row are located.

Siberia is located at the northwest part of the prison. Step inside one of the cells, close the heavy door, and it may not be surprising that visitors feel they are not alone in the dark. Meanwhile, the very thought of 5 House can leave you anxious. Here was the place where prisoners waited to die for murder.

Only one person was executed in the building that houses death row. Before that building was completed, a "death row" was located inside Cell House No. 1, commonly known as "New" Cell House, the education specialist says.

Still, troubled and guilty souls may occupy 5 House.

One woman said she heard someone pleading and begging there. The woman was born on April 13, 1951, the date of Idaho's only double execution. However, that execution took place in the No. 2 Yard, where the Idaho Botanical Garden now sits. The 5 House wasn't even built until two years after the execution. Nevertheless, the woman claimed she believed she heard the voice of Troy Powell, one of the two men executed on her birthday.

Meanwhile, the Rose Garden is a pleasant place to stop until you remember six to ten executions took place on that spot. A local reporter experienced extreme headaches while in the Rose Garden.

The weird happenings are not confined to the cells, Beierle says. A former staff member was working upstairs in the administrative offices, where echoes in the stairwell announce people coming up the steps. One day, the worker heard footsteps and called out the name of the only other staff person working downstairs. No response. When the staff member went downstairs and asked the worker why they didn't answer her, the other worker stated they had been seated the whole time and hadn't heard anything.

Certainly, the prison makes a perfect place for the spirits of those who may not be at rest after lives of crime. Built in 1870, the Old Idaho Penitentiary held almost 13,000 prisoners over the course of its 101 years as a functioning prison. Inmates constructed many of the buildings at the prison, which housed many of the state's most notorious criminals.

The historic site was featured in the "Ghost Adventures" television program on the Travel Channel Network.

With all the reported inexplicable incidents, Amber

Beierle admits to uneasiness at night.

"I relate that more to understanding the history of the site and what actually happened here, and when you couple knowledge with being on an historic site at night, you're going to get heebie jeebies. My skepticism aside, I believe that everyone has a unique and real experience here. Sometimes it's ethereal, sometimes it's educational, and hopefully, more than anything, it's engaging and contemplative."

For more about the Old Idaho Penitentiary go to www.history.idaho.gov.

SCHUBERT THEATER IN GOODING

For more than a decade eerie phenomena have been seen, discussed and investigated in Gooding, Idaho. One location is the Gooding Theater, which is also known as the "Schubert Theater."

In 2003, a group known as Ghosts in Idaho investigated the theater. According to its website, idahohauntings.com, the owner at the time said he dreamed of a woman in a white dress who told him to buy a theater. He found one in Gooding. After entering the building, he knew this was the theater the lady wanted him to purchase. Once remodeling started, his daughter reported small floating orbs all around her in the air and strange things began to happen.

The Schubert Theater is an historical and opulent building with lion heads, intricate moldings, elaborately painted art deco designs on the lobby ceiling, and large vintage paintings in the art deco style on canvas on the theater walls. It is listed on the National Register of Historic Places.

In the early days, the theater was reportedly said to be used by the Gooding and Schubert families to entertain high society guests from all over the world, and on special events the usherettes wore formal dresses, escorted their guests to their seats and bowed as they left to seat the next guest. Mrs. Schubert, who lived upstairs, would come down in her gown and jewels as hostess for the evening. Famous people attended these special events, which happened as late as the 1950s.

The present owners of The Schubert Theater, Charmianne (Charmy) and Lonnie LeaVell have not seen anything unusual — yet. Renovation of this jewel back to its former glory is of prime importance to them. Who knows?

Maybe the ghostly inhabitants will like the renovations and show themselves again.

THE BLIND MAN'S DOG
by Giselle Jeffries

Samuel and I sat on the couch listening to music from his radio. The mood created was calm, quiet, and relaxing. I lay next to him, my head on his lap and his hand resting on the back of my neck. I heard Samuel's heart slow and felt his body unwind from today's walk in the park. We were falling asleep, Samuel's dark glasses still over his eyes. We stayed like that for a couple hours. A peaceful moment we both enjoyed.

Then, an unnatural silence washed over us and woke me. Even the music had ceased. All I could hear through the open window was the small breeze blowing through the trees. Everything else went dead silent. The annoying fly stopped buzzing, the neighbor's cat stopped crying, the frogs stopped croaking, and the crickets stopped singing. I lifted my head and Samuel's hand slid down toward my back. I moved my ears, searching for the sound of another animal. Nothing. Something was wrong.

I sniffed the air for anything that would give me a clue, but everything appeared normal. Staying still, I concentrated on sensing whatever caused the other animals to go quiet. I lay there for what seemed like forever when the air in the room got colder, carrying with it the smell of death and decay. I turned my head toward the door and then to the window. Something was coming. Next to me, Samuel's body shivered and the hairs on his arm stood up. I looked to make sure he was still asleep. As I turned back to the door, I saw from the corner of my eye a dark figure come through the wall. I leaped off the couch, Samuel's arm falling to his side, and prepared myself to attack. But I was caught off guard by the strange appearance of the man before me.

He was dressed in a black cloak that trailed on the floor. A half moon-shaped amulet with red stones hung from a long chain around his neck. His head was turned down, the hood covering half his face and shadowing the rest.

The man glided toward me. He was only a few feet away when I snapped back to attention, remembering my duty to Samuel. I hunched my shoulders and growled. The man didn't stop. He didn't show any fear. So I launched myself at him, my teeth exposed and ready to sink into whatever part of his body I could get a hold of. Grabbing me with cold hands, he tossed me a few feet away like I was nothing but a rag doll. I barely made a noise as I hit the carpet by the bookshelf.

Rolling onto my feet, I jumped at him again, letting out a snarl and drool. With a wave of his hand, I ran into an invisible barrier and fell back with a thud. As I got on my feet, I realized there was no way I was going to win a fight against this man who floated across the floor.

Not knowing what else to do, I started barking for Samuel to wake, but he didn't move. The man, now standing over Samuel's sleeping body, placed his right hand a few inches from Samuel's face. A silver mist floated out and was absorbed into the man's palm.

The man folded his hands in front of himself and turned to face me. He lifted his head and the first thing I noticed was hollow eyes. His skin was wrapped around his bones so tight and transparent it appeared not to even be there. I stopped barking, finally realizing who stood before me. Then he bowed his head and turned to walk back through the wall.

I ran over to Samuel, but I already knew what I would find. I sat on the couch next to his body and howled my lament, which woke the neighbors who were now banging

The Blind Man's Dog

on the door and yelling from their rooms for me to shut up, but I wouldn't. I couldn't. Samuel was dead.

DEAD MAN'S SHOES
by Patricia Santos Marcantonio

Silver City, Idaho 1863

William Manford held onto the handful of mud. Father McFallen motioned to the open grave. Reluctantly, William threw the mud onto the coffin holding his wife Irene. He cursed her for leaving him to cook his own dinner, wash his clothes, and sleep alone on cold nights. He spun around and walked briskly down the hill, not waiting for the priest to finish the service.

Once the funeral was completed, the small gathering started back down toward Silver City. Their boots made deep prints in the April muck.

Constance Hawker, a robust woman who cooked at the Idaho Hotel, pulled up her skirt to keep it dry. "Poor Irene. I know influenza killed her, but living with that miser all those years is what really put her in the grave."

Betsy Hillard, the slight wife of a luck-poor miner, nodded. "If William Manford had a heart, it was Irene. Now that heart is six foot under."

They watched the new widower walk ahead of them.

"He did give her beautiful shoes to wear to heaven." Constance said.

"Yes, he did. But he's still the meanest man in Silver City," remarked Betsy.

William Manford did not have the look of a mean man. His eyes were blue as the Idaho sky after an unforgiving winter. He carried himself proud, but without swagger.

One foot ahead of the other, he walked in straight

lines, something difficult to accomplish when there were few straight roads in the busy mining town of Silver City. He had opened his shoe-making business on Washington Street after his gold claim failed to produce anything but an injured knee. The spring influenza that killed Irene rolled over the mountains like a dismal fog.

For William, the only shoemaker within two hundred miles, the sickness became a strike richer than any gold or silver vein found in the Owyhee Mountains that surrounded the town. The twelve cemeteries in the area saw three or four funerals a day. And everyone wanted dead man's shoes to bury their beloved in style.

Although families had little money for flour or beef, they came up with six dollars for shiny new shoes for kin's burials. To keep up with the demand, William worked eighteen hours every day. Town residents passing his shop often saw the lanterns glow late into the night. He bent over his workbench, cutting away at the precious leather, sewing, and tapping nails. No one denied the quality of the shoes, which often were displayed in his shop window. Despite an inventory of many sizes, some of the shoes did not quite fit the deceased. As a result, it was not unusual for the living to cut off toes to make sure the dead wore new leather into the ground.

When mourners complained of his prices, William muttered in reply, "That leather don't just fly to Silver City. It has to be brought in from Boise City by mule."

The day after Irene wore her own dead man's shoes into the earth, William had not once thought of her. He was thirty-five when he married Irene Dublin. At age twenty-nine, she was considered the oldest old maid in town. She had met him at a July Fourth dance. William was tired of being lonely, and Irene wanted to get away from her brother who was even more ornery.

Irene had a sturdy waist and a face that looked like saddle leather from helping at her brother's livery. While she had little to be happy about, Irene smiled most days and took the Bible seriously, especially the part about doing unto others. Unable to have children, she became mother to the neglected and poor young'uns who needed bread and milk when their miner fathers spent money on the easy houses and liquor. The kids knew they had to sneak over to the Manford House while William was at his shop, otherwise they got a door slammed on them instead of a slice of bread or container of milk.

At night, Irene served supper and a smile to her husband, which he never returned. So were the days in their four-year marriage. Now, she had passed.

The day after the funeral, William added ABSOLUTELY to the already displayed NO CREDIT sign. He shaved his heavy beard. He began seeing a hostess with flame-colored hair called Rosie Bell who sold dances for twenty-five cents at the Lost Miner Salon. She also sold more intimacies in her shack. Given the money coming in from dead man's shoes, he had plenty to spend on Rosie Bell.

While William appreciated what people paid for his dead man's shoes, he thought the tradition stupid. He believed death was just an eternal blackness like the mountainside when the lights in town all had extinguished. William was convinced that when he went into the ground, his feet could be dirty and his toenails long, and it would not make any difference. He would be dead and that was that.

Irene had held no such beliefs. The night before she died she had asked for black high-rise boots. Her body made smaller by illness, she seemed to float on the sheets soaked from fever.

"William," she whispered, "I want to meet my maker wearing good shoes. That way I can walk with pride into heaven, if He will allow me."

"You'll get your shoes, Irene," he had replied. It was the closest he had ever come to declaring any feeling for her. As she lay on their table the night before the burial, he put her feet in the best pair he had in the shop. To make up for the extravagance, he bought a simple stone that stated her name and the day she died. He was saving money for a new sewing machine to make more shoes.

The influenza that had taken so many in Silver City in March and April began to subside in the middle of May. At least, that was the observation of Doc Morrow, who drank more than a few beers in the Lost Miner Bar to forget the mortality he had witnessed.

"Silver City should start to live again," Doc Morrow said to William and John Casey, the undertaker, who made furniture when he was not making coffins.

"Well, there goes our fortunes, William," said John who looked ill even when he was well. His eyes were forever red rimmed and his face ashen. "I was hoping to save enough to leave this place and see San Francisco before I die. Now, the farthest I will make it is Ruby."

"John, you cannot save money at all because you are a bad gambler," said Doc Morrow, a tall man made even taller by his stovepipe hat.

"I knew it was too good to last." William shook his head and left.

On his way home, he met Father McFallen on Jordan Street, the main road in Silver City. "How are you, William?"

"How do you think, Priest?"

"I have not seen you in church."

"Irene was responsible for God." William did not slow

his stride.

Unlike the coffin maker, William could afford a trip to San Francisco. Hidden at his shop were hundreds of gold pieces, but he would stay put. He had a good business in Silver City and would remain there until the silver and gold ran out, and people stopped wanting good shoes for the living or the dead.

As he did most nights, William knocked at Rosie Bell's shack while he jiggled the coins in his pocket to pay for her favors. Rosie Bell answered, her red hair long and curly about her chubby face. She smiled for him, one of the few people who did, but William knew she was anticipating the money he would leave behind.

"Well, close the door. It's cold outside." Rosie Bell wrapped the thin shawl around her curvy body squeezed into a chemise and drawers. Both underpinnings were gray from her poor washing habits. Her lips were sloppy red as if she had kissed a bleeding animal. On a hook near her bed hung the thing she loved most in the world, a large velvet hat with purple ostrich feathers.

Williams licked his lips at the sight of the woman so different from his dead wife. Irene had been built like a young boy, but Rosie Bell had hips wide as a chair and a bosom that seemed to heave like thawing ground.

"I wish I was in San Francisco," she sighed.

"What's there?" William said.

"It is just not here. So where's my money?"

The next morning, a young woman with a black shawl over her head entered William's shop. Her simple brown dress shined from wear and carried a thick hem of mud. When she removed the shawl, he breathed with pleasure. Black hair glistened about a face both angelic and strong. She faintly smelled of lavender water. She had recently cried, but the tears did not make her appearance haggard. Instead her eyes glowed like a creek reflecting the sky.

"Mr. Manford, I am Mary Riggins. My father and husband have died in our cabin to the north of town. The influenza struck one and then the other." Her voice sounded steady.

"I'm supposing you want a pair of new shoes to bury them in?"

"Yes, sir."

"That will be six dollars for each pair."

"But I have no money. There is just me and my young son." She pointed to a ten-year-old boy who waited outside the shop. The youngster wore rags that only resembled pants and a shirt. His face was clean, but his hands crusty with dirt. The woman smiled at the boy and turned back to William. "We've been eating dandelions and squirrels. You see, the claim my husband and father worked bore no riches. There was only hard work. Their mine caved in on them, and they escaped only to die in bed."

"You can sell their tools."

"They were lost in the mine. I have nothing, but if you give me time, I will pay what I owe. I wrote my uncle and he is sending money through Wells Fargo so that my son and I can join him in Boise City. He also offered to pay for the funeral, but it will take three weeks for the money to arrive."

William spit on the wood floor. "I've heard worse tales."

"Please, the county is going to bury my husband and father the day after tomorrow. They did not have much in life. Let me give them something in death."

William pointed to his ABSOLUTELY NO CREDIT sign. Then he smiled crooked as the windiest street in town. "Sister, you might go sell yourself on Becker Street to raise money. Who knows, I may be your first customer."

Mary put her small hand to her mouth in disgust. She straightened. "I beg you to help us. Whatever good you do will come back to you tenfold, I promise."

"I don't need promises, sister. I need money. Give me my twelve dollars and you will get your dead man's shoes. If you cannot pay now, our business is ended. Leave or I will call Sheriff Jackson to run you out."

Slowly, the woman replaced the shawl over her head, as if she had lost another family member to death. William returned to finishing a new pair of shoes. When he looked up, the woman had not moved, but stared at him.

"You still here?" he said.

"This evil you showed us will also come back to you." She turned, her small heels tapping on the wood floor.

"That woman must think I give a damn."

In the evening, he skipped his supper and walked to the Lost Miner and to find Rosie Bell. On his way over, he purchased a silk fan in Chinatown for the whore, and thought about Mary Riggins. The smell of the lavender water was in his nostrils in spite of the thick odor of smoke, stale beer, and bacon grease in the bar. Bartender George McReedy had a smile for anyone with money.

"Give me a beer, George," William said.

"Coming right up." For all his faults, the bartender did not skimp on the beer.

"So where is Rosie Bell tonight? I want to talk mining with her." William sipped his beer without expression.

"She left early this morning with a gambler who had ruffles on his shirt. Now I am short one hurdy-gurdy girl."

"Give me another drink." William gripped the glass tighter. "Stupid no-good whore." He left the fan on the bar. Monday morning, William woke early and walked to breakfast at the Idaho Hotel.

John Casey tipped his black hat as he drove past in a simple wagon reserved for paupers who were buried on the county dole. In back of the wagon were two coffins of the cheapest wood. Walking behind were Mary, who wore the same brown dress, and the boy who had on a cleaner shirt and pair of pants.

William did not remove his hat, but only shrugged. "I hope she changes her mind about being a hostess. She would make a goodun." His smile was thick with lust.

As if she had heard, Mary looked at him, but her shawl concealed her lovely face.

She stopped and pointed a finger, as if accusing him of a crime, then lowered her hand and walked on.

His breakfast was calling.

After returning to work, William tried to focus on the dead man shoes he was making for the Mayor's son who had fallen off of a horse and broken his neck. But he thought of Irene, Rosie Bell, and Mary Riggins. He thought of his mother who had run off when he was six, leaving him with a father who loved to beat William almost as much as drink liquor. He tapped away at the shoes. Women do nothing but leave. They ain't nothing but trouble. I am better off without them. It don't pay to care about anybody.

The shoemaker rarely dreamed, but that night he did. Under a sky of cobalt and clouds, he walked to the cemetery. The priest recited words at a gravesite. His mouth moved, but no words came out. Wearing a white chemise, bloomers, and red slippers, Mary Riggins stood beside him. She looked down into the grave. Contentment made her face even more lovely. Bewildered by Mary's reaction, he also looked into the hole. At the bottom, he saw himself in a cheap coffin. His feet were covered in his best pair of dead man's shoes, shiny and tight. Suddenly, he was in the grave. Above him Mary smiled with red eyes.

William startled awake. He tore off the blanket. He wore dead man's shoes.

"I must have got drunk last night and put them on." He tried to untie the shoes, but the laces were like strings of iron.

"Somebody must be playing a trick on me. I ain't dead yet." He stomped to his workbench and cut at the leather, nicking his feet as he peeled the shoes off and threw them in the stove. He cursed because he could not sell the shoes to anyone else. He poured cold water into the basin and put his face in, as if to wake from a dream. And for a moment, he questioned what had happened, but his feet were bloody and bare. He dressed and went to work. Later at night, he pulled the shades and drank a bottle of whiskey. He fell back on his bed located in the rear of the shop. In the morning, he wore another pair of dead man's shoes. When he tried to take them off, some of his skin came off, too. He screamed so hard Sheriff Johnson knocked.

"You alright in there, William? The whole town can hear you yelling."

"Leave me alone, Sheriff. I just had a bad dream."

Sheriff Johnson left as William returned to removing the shoes, which he also burned once they were off his feet.

"That Mary Riggins cursed me." He swallowed air.

He rushed out the door, but had to go slow because each step felt as if he walked over the tips of the sharp mountain range. He limped to the general store. Mrs. Richard Stone, a woman short as a child, knew everyone in town and in the hills because they had to come to her for their necessities.

"Do you know Mary Riggins?" Williams said. The pain in his feet caused his scowl to deepen.

"Oh, yes, they had a cabin up north. Poor soul lost her husband and father in one day." Mrs. Stone had to use a step stool to reach the top of the counter.

"Never mind that, I have got to find her. Where is her cabin?"

As she talked, she made sales to children looking for hard candy. "She is gone, William. Her uncle came and got her and the boy. They left yesterday."

"But where?"

"Who knows? You need any supplies?"

He did not answer and went to look for himself. He met an old miner who had known the family and directed him to the cabin, which sat one-half mile up the mountain. William found it sadly abandoned. Tipped over chairs. Dust over a nicked bureau. The smell of dead animals. Mice droppings. On the bare bed springs lay the brown dress Mary had worn into his shop.

Returning to town, William could no longer feel his feet. They have been numbed by all the pain. Blood began to drip out of his shoes. He ignored the confused looks of people as his left a trail of bloody footprints along the boardwalk that ran in front of the businesses on Jordan Avenue. Back at his shop, he tapped at more shoes and drank a pot of coffee so that he would not sleep. But by three in the morning he laid his head down on the workbench. He awoke the next morning wearing another pair of dead man's shoes.

Every morning for the next week, William awoke wearing dead man's shoes. Each pair was more difficult to remove than the last. He stopped going to the Lost Miner to drink, or to the hotel for dinner. His face turned thin and yellow. His feet were patched, and raw. He had cut down to the bone in some places to free his feet from the shoes.

After the second week, he awoke, again wearing

another pair. William began to laugh at his predicament and could not stop until his gut ached. "If I stop laughing I will go mad," he said through cracked lips.

Staring at the shiny leather shoes on his feet, he knew what he had to do.

The ax lay in the back of his shop where he had used it to cut wood two days before.

One by one, he cut off the dead man's shoes and his feet. His screams drew half the town to his shop. Constance Hawker, his wife's old friend, found him first on her way to work at the hotel. She fainted.

Sheriff Jackson pushed his way through the crowd, which was easy because the man was over six feet tall. "God Almighty" was all he could say.

Doc Morrow was seeing to an old woman in the town of Ruby one mile away. By the time he arrived, William was pale from the loss of blood he had left outside with the shoes and his feet.

"I am free," William repeated until the doctor gave him laudanum more to quiet the ravings than the pain. The shoemaker died an hour later.

The townspeople of Silver City sighed collectively and more than a few admitted their dislike for the man. A sack of gold coins was found in a strongbox under William's bed by Sheriff Johnson, who was looking for clues for his strange behavior. The mayor suggested the money go to the county to pay for burials of the indigent, that is after the sum to buy a simple funeral for the benefactor.

On a summer day when the Owyhee Mountains burned gold from the sun, William Manford went into the dirt beside his wife Irene. No one came to see him off. In the coffin lay William Manford's body, a grimace still on his face. And next to the stumps where his feet used to be were the dead man's shoes.

His shop was boarded up because no one wanted to follow William into the insanity that had claimed him.

But on the days when the moon rested and the mountainside was dark as pity, the shop windows glowed at night as if William still sat at his workbench making shoes for the dead. While the lights could be accounted for by squatters, the fresh bloody footprints over the boardwalk were more difficult to explain by the people of Silver City.

In the end, not a soul even tried.

SCALLOPED EDGES
by Sherry Schubert McAllister

Neither blowing snow nor frost on windowpanes blocked the light that swirled shadows of a framed mirror's scalloped edges around the walls of the second-story bedroom. Two more streaks followed rapidly and disappeared, taking the faces in the mirror with them. Shouts of "Get out! Leave me alone! Go a ... waayyy!" escaped to the bedroom below.

"I'll go," drowsy Jim whispered to his wife. "It's my turn."

Daughter Jenny had not surprised them with a midnight announcement of spectral invasion for many months. Jim took the steep, shallow steps by twos in the old family farmhouse northwest of Twin Falls. He found his daughter as expected, staunchly positioned in front of her antique dresser, fists clenched, face flushed, and tears streaming. He scooped her up and held her close. "It's okay now, Kitten. Daddy's here. What happened?"

Between wiping her eyes and snuffling her nose, she managed to say, "They came again, Daddy, just like always. First the shadows, and then the faces in the mirror. I tried to make them go away."

The young farmer began the ritual that guided the pair through many such frightful nights. They rapped on the mirror, tromped around the bed to unsettle any hidden spooks, and shooed the apparitions out the window, calling, "No ghosts allowed." Then he bounced his daughter onto the bed. "Now that we've chased the spirits away, what else is bothering you?"

"Snow. The school bus will get stuck and I'll freeze to death." The child had discovered the perils of winter storms during her first school year.

Jim stifled a chuckle, knowing that a simple "you'll be fine" was not what his daughter wanted. He took a small blanket from the dresser. "This looks like my great-great-aunt Loretta's lap robe." He spread the musty covering on top of the bed and sat beside Jenny. The thick blanket of Sunbonnet Sues silhouetted on a buttery yellow background warmed the room. Jim enfolded Jenny's hand into his and they traced the curves of scalloped edges with their fingers.

"Loretta had a dimple in her cheek just like yours. She used to sleep in this bedroom, too, before children rode to school in warm buses. To keep toasty on wintry days, her mother heated a brick on the wood stove, wrapped this quilt around it, and carried babe and bundle out to the canvas-covered, horse-drawn school wagon.

"Children placed warm bricks on the wagon's bed, put their feet up on them, and wrapped heavy blankets around their legs. At Lincoln School, a janitor carried the bricks to the furnace room to reheat them for the trip home. One particularly stormy day, that ride turned into an adventure. The road drifted shut a mile from here. The children were just like you — afraid they would freeze to death. They wrapped their lap robes tight and huddled together against the elements, waiting to be rescued."

Jim glanced at Jenny's saucer eyes. "When Loretta didn't return home on time, her father enlisted the help of his old plow horse Jumbo. That giant horse was so big a saddle wouldn't cinch around him, so Loretta's father threw a blanket across his wide back, bridled him, and stood on the corral fence to mount. The huge beast lowered his head into the storm and blew frosty donuts in the air with each

Scalloped Edges

plodding step."

Jenny relaxed.

"They found the wagon with its shivering passengers. Her father wrapped Loretta in this very quilt, threw her across Jumbo's back, and headed home. After a cup of oats for the horse and a cup of hot chocolate for Loretta, she admitted she was glad to have that quilted blanket."

Jim turned to his sleepy girl. "If you ever get stuck on your way home from school, Daddy will come save you, too ... but I'll use my tractor."

"Can we name it Jumbo?"

Jim covered his daughter in the scalloped quilt. "You bet!"

When he crawled back in bed beside his wife Anne, she mumbled, "What was it this time?"

"The usual. Shadows on the walls, faces in the mirror, and an overactive imagination spooked by the storm." He didn't think to mention the sudden appearance of Sunbonnet Sue.

While Anne used warm milk and song to calm their daughter, Jim secretly enjoyed the opportunity to pass along family lore. He loved the tales learned from his grandfather.

He relished the time he and Jenny spent sharing stories, practicing an oral tradition fading as quickly as the shadows from her room. A lifetime of yarns awaited spinning.

One occasion for storytelling occurred when Jenny turned eight. A newly built school caused anxiety over separation from her friends. When screams summoned her father, they performed the usual ritual. Jim found a postcard on her dresser that sparked a tale. The card was yellowed, its scalloped edges frayed, and its postmark from Iowa dated 1912.

Jim read the scrawl.

*To my dearest friend Lena, I know you
will be happy in your new home in Idaho.
Write me every week. Don't forget
those who love you more than anything.
We'll never forget you.*

Mildred.

  He used the old note to launch into the story of his great-grandparents. They moved from the Midwest in the early days of the Twin Falls Tract searching for a new life. They came by train and brought seed money, tools, and one piece of furniture—the chest of drawers with its mirror framed in scalloped edges, hand-hewn by her father as a wedding gift.
  "Lena had a square jaw and high cheekbones—like yours. She left eleven brothers and sisters, a town full of friends, and a familiar way of life for a dusty plot of high desert sagebrush. Lonesome for a time, she finally realized new friends, as well as the old friends, would enrich her life." Jim smiled at his daughter. "You'll make friends at your new school, too. You can call your old ones anytime you want." At his daughter's yawn, Jim returned to his bedroom without asking where Jenny found the old card.
  Later came the tender age of braces and blemishes, which precipitated midnight frights and one of Jim's favorite stories.
  Shrieks of "Go away!" caused him to bound upstairs to find his daughter in tears before the mirror. Jenny encouraged their knocking on the glass together, but resisted his attempts to shoo or stomp on the floor.
  "What brought this on?" Jim asked.
  "The shadows and faces came. When they left, all I could see was ugly me in the mirror," she cried.
  "What makes you say a thing like that?"

Scalloped Edges

His preteen daughter covered her mouth self-consciously. "My braces, Daddy. I look horrible."

Jim hugged Jenny. "You are as cute as ever, and your friends won't even notice after your first smile. Did I ever tell you about my grandmother Claire?"

From the dresser, Jim picked up a small wooden box decorated with scallops etched around its edges. He wrinkled his nose at the fusty smell and peeked at the blue stone inside.

"Claire had blue eyes just like yours, and the determination to go with them. She was a town girl from a good family who married my grandfather Carl over her parents' objections. 'Don't come crawling back when times get tough,' they warned. 'Live with the choices you've made.'

"Farming in the Magic Valley was good to them, but for a few years between the two world wars, hard times shook the valley. The bottom fell out of the potato market. Farmers dumped their worthless tubers into the canyon. Carl's family ate potatoes all winter long. Claire fixed them every way she could: mush for breakfast, soup for lunch, and boiled for dinner, with chips of meat only once a week. She never complained, just did what had to be done.

"Come Christmas, Claire scrimped to save egg money to buy each child a fresh orange so there would be something under the sagebrush tree that year. On Christmas morning, this small box lay beside the fruit, and inside, a tiny bright blue stone hung from a dime store chain — like the one tucked in here.

"Carl fastened the necklace around Claire's neck and told her she looked as young and beautiful as the day they married." Jim tilted his daughter's chin upward. "It takes a long time and hard work for a young woman to grow into her beauty, but you will."

Jenny regarded her father skeptically. "Daddy, I love

your stories. Are any of them true?"

"I tell them exactly the way I heard them." Jim smiled as he placed the blue gem back in its box.

The last time that Jim heard another muffled scream and took the stairs by twos again. Jenny stood in front of the mirror.

"Sorry, Dad. I didn't mean to wake you. I'm old enough now to handle these haunts."

"What brought this on tonight?"

"Nerves. I'm going on my first date Saturday."

"Should I be worried?"

"No. We'll be with a group at Porters' harvest party, bobbing for apples and roasting marshmallows after a hayride—like when you were a kid."

Jim laughed. "You have nothing to be nervous about. Wear that beautiful smile of yours." He removed a dress covering the mirror. "This reminds me of one my sister Janet used to wear. She had a pretty smile, too, and a birthmark just below the collarbone."

"You mean Aunt Julie?"

Jim shook his head, then hesitated, unprepared to tell this story. "No. Janet was my baby sister. She died young." He held up the dress—a pretty garden of rosebuds with dainty scallops around the sleeves, neck and hem. "She loved this dress. She wore it the night she became engaged."

"Tell me about her."

"Janet was a firecracker, always getting into trouble. I remember when Evel Knievel came to town in '74 to jump the Snake River Canyon in a steam-powered skycycle, we perched on the roof of our house, binoculars to our eyes, like a flock of birds. A portable radio described the event. Next thing we knew, it was over. Knievel crashed in the canyon. Janet, disappointed, threw herself backwards and slid toward the edge of our steep roof."

"Is that what killed her?" Jenny asked.

"No. Our father caught her by the ankle before she fell off, but not before bumping her head. We teased her about who was craziest that day — Janet or Knievel. She died in an accident a few weeks later on the north side of the canyon. Father always believed that knock on the noggin clouded her judgment."

"Dad, you've never talked about her. I'm sorry if you lost a sister," Jenny said. "I understand now why climbing on the roof and going to the north side are off limits. But you taught me how to take care of myself. I don't plan to fall for the first guy who comes along." She kissed her father on the forehead. "Good night, Dad."

Choosing not to reveal the whole truth, Jim descended the stairs. In her slide down the roof, Janet's blouse rode up revealing a tummy ripe with child. Her condition catapulted the family into conflict. Defiant, Janet took up with a rough crowd. One night she slipped into the river near Pillar Falls and drowned. The community buried three that autumn: Janet, her unborn child, and later her fiancé. When he learned of their deaths and was denied leave, he walked straight out of the Vietnamese jungle into enemy fire.

During all the nights of Jenny's terrors, Jim knew that the swirling shadows were cast by high beams of vehicles racing along the country road. Phantoms in the mirror were reflections of Jenny's fears. But he could not explain the appearance of odd bits of family mementos at those times.

Three nights later, a rotating blue light splayed shadows onto the living room walls where Jim and Anne awaited Jenny's return from the hayride. Jim opened the door and met the deputy sheriff's serious gaze.

"Trouble at Pillar Falls tonight. A group went down for

a party. After last week's rain, the paths were slippery and the water ran high. No one remembers who slipped first, but five tumbled into the river like dominoes. Yours is a lucky one."

Jim's face drained. Jenny shivered, her hair and the rosebud dress still wet. She pushed past the officer and her parents, heading for the stairs. Her mother followed.

"We counted cuts, bumps and bruises, cracked ribs, and a broken arm as the kids scrambled on top of each other to get out. Porter's boy didn't make it. We'll set a net across the river down by Blue Lakes. He should surface in a few days. Usually takes three to six and a lot of patience ... but you know that."

The officer shook his head. "Darnedest thing. We found your girl a few yards down river caught in a mess of driftwood. Her skirt was stretched out tight into a perfect circle. She floated, calm as could be, not a hint of fear on her face. If she'd struggled to get free or tried to swim, she'd have been caught by an undercurrent and gone.

"Kids flock to the canyon in autumn. They don't learn from one generation to the next. They gotta lose a friend before it hits home that the river is no amusement park ride. By God's grace, you are blessed tonight."

Jim thanked the deputy and rushed upstairs. He met Anne leaving Jenny's room. "How is she?" he asked.

"Cold and damp, but physically unhurt. She wrapped that crazy baby quilt around her shoulders and won't budge from staring into the mirror. I'll heat some milk."

Jim entered quietly. "Kitten?"

"Three pairs of hands weren't enough to save Janet."

"What?"

"But four pairs of hands reached down to save me. I'm sorry, Daddy. I didn't know the hayride would be in Jerome or that we'd build the campfire in the canyon. I tried not to go down, but ..."

"Shhh. I'm sorry I wasn't there to save you."

"They did. All four of them. I know now that every story you've told me is true. I saw them. Loretta, Lena, Claire, and Janet were there tonight ... by the river. They pulled me to a safe place and stretched my skirt out to hold me up until help came. They are here now, I feel it."

Despite Jim's disbelief, Jenny persisted. "I never understood where those things came from until now. Those spirits appeared not to haunt me, but to help me."

After Jim left, Jenny stared into the mirror, summoning her guardians. She closed her eyes, and when she opened them, they were there—but not in the mirror. Four women surrounded her. Four hands rested on her shoulders, and four reflections joined hers in the mirror. Jenny compared their faces and her own. Lena's set jaw and high cheekbones, Loretta's dimple, and Claire's determined blue eyes. Janet's smile was hers, and the scalloped neck of the party dress exposed their identical birthmarks.

At the flash of approaching lights, Jenny cried, "Don't go! Stay! Please stay."

Shadows swirled, spiriting away the faces in the mirror.

FACES IN THE WATER
by Patricia Santos Marcantonio

Lt. Joshua Morton cursed his need for excitement, love of dime store novels and joining the Calvary. All he had discovered in the year since he put on the blue uniform was the true color of sagebrush. It was a greenish gray.

Lately, he wished that he still worked for the newspaper back in Boise. But no. He wanted to live life instead of write about it. Unfortunately, saddle sores and bad food dominated the life he chose.

The crunch crunch crunch of his horse's iron shoes on the snow mocked Joshua as he and the other soldiers rode toward the Snake River. The air felt like he breathed in cold needles. But the miserable conditions were not complete without Capt. Thurston Walsh, who rode in front of him.

Walsh was built like a sack of grain. He was a man with a heavy mustache and red cheeks even in the summer time who disliked anyone who didn't believe what he did, or looked like he thought they should. In other words, Walsh hated everybody, especially Indians.

"Godless dirty savages," Walsh had frequently told Joshua. "All they believe in is the Earth and sky and talking animals. And they are standing in the way of the white man's progress. They do not deserve to live." Joshua never argued with Walsh. He'd sooner be able to change the color of the sky than the captain.

Their patrol had been given the task of quelling an uprising of Indians who had killed seven settlers weakened by the already unforgiving winter. The raiders had been tracked to a camp near the banks of the Snake River thirty miles from the fort. For most of their journey to the river, the captain repeated "rub them out" and "kill them all." Joshua shivered from those ravings as much as the biting wind.

As Joshua rode along his nerves fired with equal parts of fear and thrill. This was the first time he'd been assigned to track down hostiles. Most of the Indians he had encountered at the fort or on patrol did not look fierce.

When the contingent arrived near the camp, Walsh told the men to stay with the horses while he and Joshua crept close enough for a view through a spyglass. The camp consisted of nine tents pitched in the snow. Fires dotted the site.

"Sir, I do not see any warriors, just old men," Joshua whispered. "Mostly, there are women and children in the camp. Maybe fifteen of them."

"Makes no difference. They're Indians and they killed white men. We're going to attack." Walsh breathed out puffs of breath in the frigid air. His yellow teeth clamped together.

"Those women and children did not kill the settlers, Captain. We should wait for the men, capture them and return them to the fort for court justice."

The Captain didn't answer and returned to the soldiers. Mounting his horse, Walsh pulled out his weapon. "We're going to wipe them out." He kicked his horse in the sides and sped toward the camp.

The rest of the soldiers looked at each other. They were like Joshua, young and untried. They didn't know what else to do but follow. The captain rode ahead, shooting at the scampering targets. The old men yelled, the women screamed, the children cried. The bullets hit them so hard in the back they appeared yanked to the ground by unseen ropes. Even the Indian ponies cried as the Captain shot them. The animals crashed to the snowy ground in a spray of blood.

Joshua held his weapon but could not fire.

Faces in the Water

Walsh rode by Joshua, grabbed the reins of his horse and pulled his red face close. "What are you waiting for, Morton? Shoot them. That is an order."

Letting go of the reins, the Captain got down off his horse and shot an old man point blank in the head. The man went down with a thud.

Joshua turned his horse toward a group of boys and girls running toward the wide deep river some hundred feet from the camp.

"God forgive me. " Joshua fired and the children fell into the river's icy water. The air smelled of blood and gunpowder. The more he shot, the more he felt like a horseman of the Biblical apocalypse, raining down bullets and terror. When his gun clicked, the force of his deed slammed into his chest like a tree trunk.

Riding to the river bank, Joshua forced himself to look at the bodies in the water. The black hair of the children floated like river grass. Many of their eyes were open as if gazing at him.

Within minutes, the camp was cleared. Most of the Indians lay dead or dying in the snow. Joshua and the soldiers gathered in the middle of the ravaged camp, their horses creating a mist of condensation and stamping on the bloody dirt.

The Captain stood in front of them. Joshua's horror increased tenfold. Walsh's eyes were wide with an insane righteousness. Red veins popped in his eyes like thin fingers. He had the look of the man who had dipped himself in blood and wanted more.

Walsh pointed to three young soldiers, who trembled not from the cold but from all the death. "I want this place burned to the ground."

By the time they returned to the fort, Joshua had a

violent fever. He fell from his horse as soon as they entered the gates. For six weeks, he writhed under blankets made wet from night sweats. His long blond hair was matted to his forehead from the fever. For six weeks, he dreamed of what happened at the river. He dreamed of the how the women and children dropped. Their screams and chanting. He dreamed of red snow and the bodies in the water. Their eyes were white. Their hair wavered and beckoned.

For the first moments when he woke, Joshua prayed that the massacre was all a dream. But the blood on his boots, which he had not had the strength to clean, reminded him of his sins.

Greatly weakened and pale, Joshua finally returned to duty. He felt better right until the moment Capt. Walsh sent for him.

"Good to see you among the living, Morton," Walsh said.

"Thank you, sir."

"No rest for the wicked."

Joshua's heart contracted tight under his shirt and he felt himself sway.

"You sure you are well enough?" Walsh talked with spit every time he grew angry. "I hope you are not going to let me down again."

"I am fine, sir."

"We're returning to the Snake."

The name made Joshua sick.

"There have been no more raids, but a few days ago miners who passed by the area heard chanting and crying children. They got so spooked they sped out of there. I told the colonel they were crazy old coots but he says we have to check it out."

"The camp was wiped out," Joshua said. "What could

Faces in the Water

be left out there?"

"Orders are orders." Capt. Walsh dismissed Joshua with a motion of his hand.

That night, Joshua again sweated into the blankets in his bed. He dreamed again of the river but not of blood and snow. This time, he dreamed that he gazed up to the sky blue as God's eyes. Trout skidded over him and his hands clenched slick rocks. He turned his head and a beautiful Indian child held out his arms to him.

Joshua woke up gasping for air.

The next morning, they rode to the river. Joshua said nothing for the first hours but eventually had to ask. He clicked his tongue so his horse could catch up to the captain's.

"Captain, what we did at the Indian camp, "Joshua said.

"Yes?"

"Doesn't that bother you?" Maybe he was making his own confession.

"You think they have a conscious about killing those settlers? They do not even believe in God," Walsh said.

"But those women and children were unarmed."

"This is no time to doubt, Lieutenant. Just look straight ahead."

The captain speeded up his horse.

They reached their destination in the afternoon. Most of the snow had melted leaving little to show of the Indian campsite but pieces of burned wood and leather. The captain ordered Joshua to take half of the men and comb the area, and he would do the same. Joshua didn't want to but had to look down into the river water, and the source of his nightmares.

There was nothing below the surface but rocks.

Joshua was half relieved and half disappointed.

"The Indian men returned and found all the bodies.

They took them away for burial," said a solider with dark hair. "At least that's what I heard at the fort. You were at that engagement weren't you, Lt. Morton?"

"More massacre than an engagement, Private."

The soldier shrugged. "I am just happy I was not there."

After searching for hours, the soldiers met back at the abandoned camp and reported nothing. The captain said they were to stay there for the night and posted two guards. Walsh did not eat and sipped at the bottle of whiskey that he had brought.

"We have wasted our time here. Damn those miners with their stories about crying and chanting," the captain said.

The soldiers slept while the captain continued to drink. Although spring was well on its way, Joshua was still chilled and scooted nearer the fire and away from the captain. The full moon turned everything dark sepia. Joshua looked up at the lodge poles bending to and fro with the wind. The whispering night helped him fall asleep to the drunken muttering of Capt. Walsh.

Joshua sat up.

He did not know the time, but the moon was high. A sound like a rhythmic wailing of children woke him. So heartbreaking. As if all happiness in life had been crushed. The sounds came from the direction of the river. Joshua glanced around. All the other soldiers slept hard except for Capt. Walsh. He also sat up. The empty bottle fell from his hand.

"Damn them." The captain grabbed his gun. Getting up with effort, he ran toward the water.

"Captain," Joshua jumped up and followed. The children's cries became louder and louder as they neared Snake River.

Faces in the Water

    The captain reached the bank, swiveling this way and that to find the source of the weeping. Joshua arrived just in time to see children's hands jet out of the water, grab the captain's legs and tug him beneath the surface. The captain had no time to yell.

    The crying stopped.

    With small steps, Joshua got closer to the bank. He looked down and shook his head hard as if to wake up from another nightmare. Staring back at him were the faces of the Indian children lying in the water. Their bodies were uncorrupted by death and their long hair undulated like water plants. Their eyes looked like black stones. Joshua turned to run, but arms jetted out of the water and held his legs. The small hands burned his skin right through his pants. Not from heat, but with a prickling stunning cold.

    Joshua fell on his face and grabbed at the sand on the river bank but he was yanked down.

    The last thing Lt. Joshua Morton remembered was gazing up at the moon from underneath the water. Trout zipped by overhead and frogs moaned. Joshua turned his head to see the faces of those he had killed. Their eyes were now white as sour milk, and decomposition ripped at their bodies. Bubbles erupted from their noses as they chanted a victory song. Their hands held Joshua down as his lungs filled.

    Like the water children he had created, Joshua's long yellow hair floated under the water and waved to the moon overhead.

STRANGER IN A SNOWSTORM
by Loyd Bakewell

"I regret to inform you that your wife, Maggie, has been killed in a stabbing." Jason was serving in the Marines in Iraq when the chaplain showed up at the barracks. Startled, the young soldier felt tears in his eyes. Military families dread a phone call or knock at the door in wartime, fearing a loved one might have been killed. For Jason, the tables had been turned. The chaplain's hand rested on his shoulder while he regained his composure. He helped the devastated young man apply for, and receive, a hardship discharge to take care of his daughter, Tina.

Jason's mother invited him and Tina to share her home in Twin Falls, Idaho, enabling him to work and care for his little girl. Even so, throughout the next half-dozen years, his pain would not leave. Drugs and alcohol became his crutches, and these addictions consumed him. He lost his job at a sugar factory, and the courts terminated his parental rights.

By age thirty-one, Jason was a homeless veteran who had given up on life. He stood on the corner of Filer and Washington streets, holding a sign drawn on a piece of cardboard, hoping no one would recognize him. The homeless under what locals called the Singing Bridge in Rock Creek Canyon became his new family. Together, they prepared for winter, but the thought of facing Christmas without his daughter was excruciating. The bleak loneliness of each night crushed any hope of retrieving a meaningful life. He wished it would all end like a bad dream, but the night sounds of water passing over the rocks and of other homeless souls at the campsite kept him awake.

One night, as the others tossed and turned uneasily on

the camp's rocky slope, Jason thought he heard an intruder. Looking around, he met the eyes of a cat climbing out of a trash can. He relaxed back into the circle of his new family. He pulled the threadbare blanket close to calm his shivering, but bitter thoughts ate at him. *I'm so angry at the creep who stabbed my wife. How could the courts have declared me incapable of providing a home for Tina?* His stomach growled. He sat up. It was a good time to dumpster-dive behind a restaurant at the top of the canyon.

Rolling up his tattered blanket and tying it below the backpack, he slipped quietly through the sleeping forms of the camp onto the trail up the hill to Shoshone Street. Jason never knew when the restaurant would throw out leftover food, which meant this hour could deliver either a feast or nothing. If he got there after they discarded the uneaten food but before they dumped the other trash, his meal would be reasonably clean.

That night his timing was good. From the dumpster he would enjoy elegant dining without the big bucks. He withdrew a spoon and pie-tin from his backpack, and carefully transferred a piece of medium-cooked prime rib, two shrimp, French fries, and carrot cake onto his plate. He attempted to leave the remaining food as undisturbed as possible for later dumpster-divers. As he sat between the dumpster and a flour mill, the rumbling of his stomach quieted. When Jason finished eating, he wrapped his tin and spoon in newspaper and returned them to his backpack. The odors of moldy potatoes and other garbage reached his nostrils, making him realize he had become accustomed to the smell of refuse.

As Jason began the long walk back to the camp, his thoughts were intent on drinking himself to sleep. The sky emitted flurries of snow. He lowered his head, shielding himself. A customer coming out of the restaurant collided with him. "Hey bum, get out of my way," the graying man in boots and cowboy hat yelled.

"What makes you think you're any better than me?" Jason shot back. He adjusted his backpack and continued on his way, his head full of unhappiness. *People are such harsh judges of those down on their luck. I have a good reason for being homeless.*

Back at camp, Jason reclaimed his spot between two fellow panhandlers, Sam and Randy, and quickly unrolled his blanket. Wind gusts carried the heavy snowfall under the bridge. The whole camp would soon be huddled together just to make it through the night. He took a swig of whiskey, pulled the blanket over his head, and dozed.

Sometime later, Jason awakened. A five-inch blanket of snow covered him. Concerned, he fumbled inside his coat pocket for the bottle to warm up. As he attempted to shove his body upward through the snow, he slipped and was assailed by dizziness. The shadowy form of a stranger emerged from the driving snow and reached to him. Jason grabbed his hand. The young man, strong as a body builder, lifted him up.

"We have to wake the others," his rescuer said.

Jason sobered quickly.

"We'll have to hurry. This is no way to die."

As they raced to awaken everyone, the stranger moved with grace and strength. "Wake up!" Jason yelled. Only four mounds stirred. Digging in a frenzy, he scraped snow away from Sam's and Randy's heads and arms. Sam's eyes fluttered open in terror. Randy woke next. Both men tried to speak, but their words came out slurred.

Jason found a dry spot and built a fire with previously gathered wood. After carrying Sam and Randy near the heat, he and the stranger resumed their attempts to rescue the others buried in the snow.

"We need help," the stranger said.

Jason reached into his coat pocket for his cell phone. "I hope the battery is not dead," he muttered as he dialed 911. After a quick exchange of information with the police dispatcher, he announced, "Help's on the way." He thought, for the first time in a long time, I actually care whether I live or die.

Nine of the twelve members of the homeless family were soon huddled around the fire. One person at a time, Jason and the stranger were winning the battle against the storm, but it wasn't over yet. As the snowfall lightened, the two men succeeded in uncovering The Kid, a thirteen-year-old who had recently joined the family after running away from an abusive home. The half-frozen young man would not wake.

Police and paramedics arrived and began resuscitating The Kid, who soon started breathing on his own. Jason let out a whoop. All efforts went into rescuing the remaining family members. Firemen dug Old Man out of the snow with shovels, but his heart had stopped.

The stranger uncovered a woman known as Maxine. After Jason brushed snow from her nostrils, she stumbled to her feet.

While Jason answered questions for the police, he watched the stranger walk toward the street light and disappear. The police directed the ambulance driver to take Old Man's body away. The police took The Kid into child protection. A pastor of a local church announced they had set up a shelter for the survivors. Jason took a deep breath, picked up his backpack and blanket, and followed the others into the church van. When his homeless family and the rescue workers tried to make a hero of him, he protested that he hadn't done it alone.

A warm and friendly older couple welcomed them all

into the church gym with hot coffee and orange juice. The new arrivals were told they could expect a hot breakfast. Showers and clean clothing were available. The homeless women headed for the shower, while Jason and the men went directly to the hot coffee.

Jason took the near death of The Kid and the mysterious help of the stranger as a sign. It was time to stop hiding. He could stay at the homeless shelter until he beat his addictions and became a good father to Tina.

He asked a church member for a ride back to the camp. He wanted to thank the stranger. At the bridge, Jason walked toward the streetlight where he had last seen him. He looked for footprints in the snow. There were none.

PIECES OF HEAVEN CUPCAKERY IN TWIN FALLS: A MIX OF SWEET AND SPIRITS
by Patricia Santos Marcantonio

Talk to the Canary family and they've found their own piece of heaven.

Gary and Krislyn and daughter Samantha operate the Pieces of Heaven Cupcakery at 153 Main Ave. E. in Twin Falls. Look in the window of their shop and you'll see beautiful treats they bake and decorate--cupcakes, cakes, cookies and candy.

The family will also tell you that at their business, there's a mix of the sweet and the strange.

Their shop is in part of the Rogerson building, which used to be a luxury hotel in the 1900s. It now houses businesses and offices and still shows some of the original woodwork from the early days.

Gary said he had heard the building might have been haunted but didn't put stock in the stories. However, he was made a believer when they opened their business more than two years ago.

"We have had times when there were just us in the building and you can hear people talking," he said.

Samantha said it sounds like two people chatting. "You just hear it. There's something there in the hallway and it's not there when you go out to look."

Krislyn also has a story. "The other day we had a measuring cup that was in the cocoa container and I laid it on top of the lid. I went to get a bowl. When I turned around, the measuring cup was actually on the side of the container. There was no one else in the room but me and I know I didn't do it." That was the second time she had seen the measuring cup placed in that position. "I asked if (my daughter) did it and she said no she's never done it that way so that was kind of creepy."

They have also heard the sound of people walking around and other noises and creaks. "A creak that is not normal," Gary added. People tell him the place is settling but he replies it's an older building and "it's not still settling."

Where did the spirits come from? Gary heard rumors that there might have been a speakeasy in the basement during the hotel's early days. That's the only place in the building where the ex-Navy serviceman gets a creepy feeling. Mostly, the family doesn't feel threatened by the spirits, if there are any. On the contrary, "it's happy with what we are doing."

Take his story about a jar of cherries.

Gary said he and Krislyn were using cherries to decorate their baking. The lid of a jar of cherries was lying on the counter and showed spots of red cherry juice. When he turned around to replace the lid, it looked wiped clean except for a smiling face made of cherry juice. Gary and his wife asked each other if they had made the face and neither had. Gary replaced the lid and shook the jar.

"They want my wife and I to know they're here," he said.

TWIN FALLS' GHOSTLY LIBRARIAN
Twin Falls Public Library
by Bonnie Dodge

The Twin Falls Public Library is a place to encounter thousands of stories. It might also be the place to encounter a ghost.

According to local lore, there is a quiet presence among the shelves and books in the library, a feeling that one is not alone. Sudden movements and shifts in the air are common, as if someone is walking behind you, but when you turn, no one is there.

There are unexplained sounds—doors opening and closing, and footsteps—at odd moments when the library is quiet and no one is moving about, except maybe the ghost.

Some suspect the noises and sudden movements are made by the busy but benign spirit of a former and longtime librarian, who was one of the earliest directors of the library when it was built in 1939. The librarian worked at the library for thirty years. She did not marry or have family in the area, but she loved children, the library and books. In fact, the library appeared to be her life. Months after her retirement, she died.

Perhaps the librarian never moved on. Perhaps her spirit lingers in the library where she watches over unsuspecting patrons and her books.

WHERE STORIES ARE BORN
by Nadine York

What is this place? Craig stood at the top of the stairs trying to understand the floor plan in front of him. "Welcome to The Sanctuary Shelter," Kevin, the night manager, had said. Craig assumed it was a church when he checked into the basement of the white brick building three nights ago. But now nothing in the shadowy light resembled any church he'd ever seen.

He took in the imposing desk straight ahead of him. I bet no one slips past whoever sits there. To his left, eight doors lined a wide hallway disappearing into darkness. A swath of framed glass windows rose above them to meet the ceiling. Craig felt small, like on his fourth-grade field trip to the Capitol Building, looking up at its starry dome.

He was in forbidden territory and knew it.

"You can bed down anywhere here in the basement," Kevin had instructed that first night. "The upper levels are off limits. I'll put a curse on you if I find you wandering where you shouldn't be."

Craig hadn't planned to break the rules. Stepping over the flimsy rope and up the stairs past the makeshift KEEP OUT sign was a spur of the moment decision, an act of desperation — much like when he had fled Boise eighteen years before. But this time instead of running away, he was looking for a way to stay.

Outside temperatures hovered in single digits night and day with no sign of warming. What in hell possessed you to come back to Idaho, especially in January? You really are a loser, just like he always said. Craig's thoughts rolled round like a torture wheel.

For the moment, fleeing Idaho was out of the question. Yesterday's headache had persisted. His body was slipping into full-blown breakdown with chills and fever. He just wanted to sleep in a warm place, to succumb to the fever.

But Sanctuary was only a night shelter. Kevin's wake-up call would come at six. By seven everyone would have cleared out. The building would stay locked until evening again.

At four in the morning Craig dragged himself to the bathroom. He was already upstairs, heading to the main level when he heard Kevin's footsteps.

Shit! What now, smart-ass? Craig needed somewhere to hide. Standing in front of the imposing desk was no time to figure out where that place was. His eyes searched the darkness …

The shadowy ascent to the third level beyond the desk was forbidding. He turned toward a smallish side room visible by the reach of light from street lamps. Against the room's outside wall was a broad stone fireplace, cold and empty. Craig's feverish imagination conjured a roaring fire. He wanted to drop his tired bones in front of its heat and stay forever.

No hiding there. He returned to the lobby and noticed an obscure door at the top of the stairs. Was that there before? To still the uncontrollable shivers, he pulled his blanket tighter around his shoulders, and then hesitated in front the door.

"Go on, open it, chicken butt!" Joey's voice dared him. He hadn't thought of Joey for years. Within two days of returning to Boise, memories were spilling. Joey was part of the good years before Craig's father died and the Larry phase. Shit! Don't wanna think of that bastard—wish I'd been as lucky as Joey in the stepfather department.

Craig reached out and twisted the handle.

Where Stories Are Born

A closet. Kevin would find him for sure here. Pulling the door shut, he saw a ladder in the shadowy rear of the closet reaching up through a slot in the ceiling. Maybe, just maybe. With his last bit of energy, Craig pulled himself up the ladder and disappeared into the attic before giving in to delirium.

Memories swirled in a flood—images, voices, feelings buried deep under layers of time, years of wandering. Craig's body tossed and burned in sleep while his dreams spiraled in rapid twists and turns.

"Be back by six and don't let that door slam!" His mother's voice pursued him down the back stairs of their North End bungalow. He and Joey grinned, waiting for the bang and her predictable "Goddammit, Craig Allen Tucker ..." They were off and running.

"Don't cry, Mom. I'll take care of us," his boy voice whispered after the funeral, pretending braveness. "I can get a paper route." She turned her head. That began their silence, each learning to live with loss alone.

"Let go of me! Leave me alone." Eleven year-old Craig pulled away.

Larry's vice-like grip around Craig's skinny arm kept him from running. "Too bad you weren't in the car with your daddy," Larry's voice hissed. "You're just baggage for your mama and me."

Craig groaned in his sleep until escaping Larry's hold. He searched for his mother to tell her, to make her see what a bastard Larry really was. But she only said, "You don't have to call him Dad. He'll take care of us."

Craig woke from the nightmare screaming, "No!"

Surprised to feel the burn of tears, he hadn't even cried at his mother's funeral. Larry was all Craig had then, and with his mother gone, his stepfather never had to pretend niceness to the baggage—ever again.

Craig pushed away thoughts of those next three years. He had grown an armor of steely anger. Larry's final assault when Craig was sixteen caused him to bolt, and never look back. Until now.

Light came through the ventilation shaft—must be after seven, Kevin's gone.

Halfway down the ladder, dizziness overtook Craig. With sheer will he reached the closet floor before crumpling. As good a place as any. He huddled into a heap and slept.

🕷 🕷 🕷

A small hand jiggled his arm. "What are you doing in here? I been looking everywhere for you. It's time."

Time for what? He peered into serious gray eyes framed by dark bobbed hair and blunt bangs. He tried to remember if he'd seen this small girl with any of the homeless families at the shelter.

"Come on, hurry. It's time for story hour," she said as if answering the scramble in his head. Her small hands around his wrist tugged, willing him to rise.

"Story hour ...?" he mumbled.

She stopped, gripped his wrist, hesitant. She stared at him as if doubting herself, something not quite right. Her urgency returned.

"You know ... it's Saturday. Miss Laura's going to read Hans Christian Anderson today—The Little Mermaid. Let's go. It's almost ten." Before he could stop her, she opened the closet door into the lobby. He scrambled to his feet and followed.

Nothing could have prepared him. Down the stairway

to his left, sunshine poured through the glass double doors. Beyond the green lawn, a passing trolley jangled its bell. He inhaled with an audible rush. What the hell? Her insistent tug yanked his attention back.

"Jesus, this is a library!" Craig said.

"Of course, you silly ... and you better stop your swearing or I'll tell on you." Moving toward the fireplace room, the little girl chirped a greeting toward the solidly built woman behind the desk in the central lobby. "Mornin', Miss Wood!"

"Good morning, May ... Tom. Just about to begin. It's a good one today."

Craig stumbled. He looked behind himself. Tom? Who was that lady talking to?

In the fireplace room, a slender woman in front of the hearth bent over one of the children at her feet. As she stood, the hemline of her full-skirted dress rose, revealing narrow, high-buttoned, leather boots. Craig felt like he was eight, sitting next to his mother, looking at the photos of his long-dead great grandparents. "They pioneered this valley, cleared over a hundred acres," his mother's voice echoed. "You've got deep roots here."

May had already sunk cross-legged to the floor, leaving Craig standing alone.

The woman cleared her throat and nodded to him. Despite the severe high collar and sweptback hair, she radiated kindness.

"Sit down." May tugged at his pant leg.

Craig folded to the floor beside her.

"Once upon a time ..."

🕷 🕷 🕷

"I hope you'll read that one again next week too, Miss Laura," May said. "I wish I was a mermaid. I wish I lived in a big castle."

"I can tell you liked the story, May," Miss Laura said. "What about you, Tom? Can you imagine yourself being a prince?"

"What?" he stuttered. Then, as if her question pierced his fog, he exploded in frustration. "Are you kidding? What's going on here? Is this some kind of joke? I'm trying to figure out what's real and you're talking princes and fairy tales."

"Princes and mermaids are real!" May protested.

He shook his head.

"They are too! Tom. You told me so yourself. You said everything is real in the place where our dreams live. It's where stories are born. That's why we come here every Saturday. What's the matter with you anyway, Tom?" May finished.

"Stop calling me Tom! My name is Craig." He softened his voice when he saw the confusion on her face. "Look, I'm a little lost. I've never seen either of you before in my life. I don't know how I got here, but I know my name is not Tom."

The woman and girl looked at each other and back at him. Finally Miss Laura spoke. "Please forgive us. You look so much like Tom, and being with May, I naturally assumed ..."

"He is Tom!" May's voice rose.

"Tom who?"

"Tom Whitlock, you can't fool me. You're my favorite-est person in the whole Children's Home. You always walk me to the library for story time 'cause Miss Cynthia only lets me go if you agree to take me. You're an orphan, too, just like me 'cause your pa died in a tangle with a hay baler and your ma ran away with a travelin' shoe salesman. Just 'cause you're fifteen don't you even think about leaving the Home and getting a job like you've been saying, 'cause ... 'cause ..." She ended in a gulp.

The name Whitlock turned in his head. But May was more immediate. The desperation in her voice raised an old ache in his chest, like when he wanted to talk to his mom but she was too lost to hear him. He wanted May to understand.

"Listen, I'm Craig Tucker. My father died in a car accident and my mother died when I was thirteen. Her maiden name was Whitlock."

May asked Miss Laura, begging support, tears welling in her eyes. "Doesn't that make him Tom Whitlock?"

Miss Laura had been studying Craig. "No, I'm afraid not, May. You look so much like Tom Whitlock that I didn't notice that you're older than he and ... well, different — your clothes and hair." Miss Laura hesitated. "You're not from here, are you?"

"I grew up here, but I've been away for a while. Last night a shelter was in the basement of this building ... well, sort of, but different than the way it looks right now. None of these books were here. It was empty."

"You're talking crazy. It's not empty. Look!" May said, unable to keep quiet.

Craig looked toward the reading room, equally bewildered.

"May!" Miss Laura reprimanded. She turned toward Craig and explained, "It has been our library for six years now, since '05 — a gift from Mr. Carnegie. Perhaps after you left ...?"

Craig's brain felt swollen and fuzzy. The math just wasn't computing. "Six years? Since '05 ... and now it's ...?"

"Nineteen eleven, of course," May answered. "You've been away a long time. You sure look like Tom. You must be a cousin. Why did you come back? You could visit us — me and Tom — on Sundays ... at the Home ..."

"May Pickerell, you do prattle. It's rude to go on so. I

think we need to let our visitor look around on his own," Miss Laura interrupted, smiling apologetically at Craig. "Come with me now, young Miss May. I suspect we might find your Tom downstairs in the Reading Room, and I have some new books you might like to check out." She took May's hand and headed out toward the desk. "Welcome back, Craig," she said over her shoulder. "Make yourself at home."

"Oh yes! And when you come tomorrow, we can go to the park and maybe to the Natatorium." May smiled at him with the confidence of someone who makes friends, someone for whom life is an adventure.

The eastern wall of the fireplace room glowed. Craig's shirt was damp and the blanket tossed off. The fever had broken. The lobby's emptiness made him wince. Where did she go? What happened to her? He shook his head. A child named May, an orphan—like himself—but without the steel armor. A bright flame in a dark dream. A fever dream? Something in him wanted to believe that it was real, that there was something for him here. You could stay and find out. Her voice was in his head.

"I think I will," he said.

In a few hours the city's homeless would file into the basement of the old Carnegie building for shelter. Craig would find a way to slip down amongst them and blend. A night just like any other. No one would know any different, except him.

THE SPIRIT IN THE BASEMENT
by Eileen Davidson

"Mommy was really happy when Daddy built those shelves in the corner of the basement."

The reedy voice in Alan's ear startled him out of his seat, and he almost hit his head on the low beam down the room's center. He glared back at the couch where he had been sprawled to watch the final putt of the championship game, fully prepared to cuss out the neighbor's boy for sneaking into the basement again. No one was there.

Alan stared suspiciously into the corners of the room and even looked under the saggy old sofa, but found no kid. Settling back into the cushions, he was disgusted to find he had missed who'd won. A teen romance was playing.

"I helped and only cried a little when I stepped on a nail. Daddy said I was brave!"

Alan sat up and glared around the room again, but the door was shut. He could hear the comforting creak of the floor overhead as his wife Christine moved around.

"Who's there?" he whispered fiercely as his eyes darted around to spot any motion in the room. There was nothing. He flopped back into the cushions and took sharp jabs at the remote. "Seventy-six channels and still nothing on," he groused. Alan shut the set off and heaved himself to his feet to see if his wife had anything interesting planned for the evening.

"Oh, good. You're just in time to take these to the fruit room." Christine waved her hand at the dozens of Mason jars full of apricots and apricot nectar. Alan crossed the rough wood floor of the kitchen to nuzzle his wife behind the ear.

She giggled and pushed him away playfully. "I made an upside-down cake, which should be ready soon." Alan rolled his eyes and groaned like a teenager asked to clean his room. He patted his wife's bottom with a wicked grin as he turned away to put the first dozen jars into a crate.

In the basement, Alan set the box on the workbench and twisted the block nailed to the wall to release the door. The fruit room was musty; the only light hung in the center. He twisted the bulb in its socket to turn it on. He retrieved the crate and transferred jars to the shelf. As he finished, he heard the whisper again.

"Mommy loved putting apricots in here. She said it was the fruits of our labor 'cause all four of us would pick and clean and squish up the 'cots so she and Sissy could stuff them in jars. Daddy got the ones in the treetop from that weird three-leggie ladder an' Mommy let me climb up the tree just a bit to pick the middle ones."

Alan froze as he listened to the thin voice. He could picture a boy about seven years old shyly telling the story, leaning against the door and twisting the wooden spools serving as doorknobs. Alan turned slowly from the shelves and saw just that—until the child met his eyes and vanished. The empty crate crashed to the floor.

Alan poked his head out of the fruit room door and surveyed the rest of the basement. No little boys. He grabbed the box and started back to the kitchen, leaving the door open and the light on. He glanced into dim corners and behind the huge old furnace, but saw only cobwebs and dust. In the kitchen, he refilled the crate as Christine washed pots and bowls.

"Honey, have you ever heard voices in the basement?" he hesitantly asked. Christine dropped a kettle back into the soapy water and whirled around. He stared solemnly into her wide eyes. Her reaction was not comforting. He wanted her to tell him it was just his imagination.

"The boy in ragged overalls outside the fruit room? You saw him too?"

"He's been telling me how happy his mother was to have the shelves and how the whole family helped pick apricots."

Christine wound her soapy arms around Alan's neck and hugged him. "I'm so glad it's not just me. I thought I was losing my mind hearing that whisper and seeing his figure at odd moments. Wait, you actually understood what he said? It sounded like voices from another room to me." She let go of her husband and stepped back. "Do you think he's still there?"

They crept down the stairs together and entered the fruit room. For a few moments nothing happened.

"Mommy wanted to fill every single shelf. We died before she could. Daddy and Sissy cried for days and days. Then Daddy picked the prettiest yellow rose off the little bush out front and put it up there." Alan and Christine turned slowly to see his solemn face staring at the top shelf behind their heads. "It was the only shelf Mommy didn't have all used up." The child vanished.

The couple looked at each other. Alan reached up and felt around, wincing when his finger felt something sharp. He pulled down a rose, long dead and fragile. Attached was a yellowed card with spidery writing:

"My beloved Wife.
You filled my Heart."

They carefully returned the dried flower to the shelf. The yellow rosebush is now a tree.

SHADOWS AT THE SIDEWINDERS BAR
The Sidewinders Bar - Murtaugh
by Patricia Santos Marcantonio

Sheila Huizar wants to know who is haunting her bar.

Out of the corner of her eye, Sheila often sees shadows of a figure moving from door to door at her business, the Sidewinders in Murtaugh. The stereo system has been known to suddenly erupt "full bore," although no one else is in the place. Doors open by themselves and then shut just as mysteriously.

Her bartenders hear thumping upstairs when no one lives on the second floor. They hear piano music but there is no piano in sight. A customer reported seeing a man in an overcoat and black hat standing in a corner.

The building does have a long history in the small town. Constructed in 1908 as a general store, it became a Model T repair shop, and has been a bar since 1947. Sheila purchased the bar in 2002, but has worked there since 1995.

The strange happenings at Sidewinders have unnerved some of her employees, Sheila says. "A couple of them have been pretty skittish."

"I'm not scared of ghosts and I don't know if that's even what it is," she says.

If they are ghosts, Sheila is curious about them. In a box in the basement, she found two antique portraits of a man and woman. No one knows their identities, including the old-timers she asked. Were they the store owners whose spirits stuck around? Who knows? Sheila Huizar is fascinated with the questions.

The next time you visit the Sidewinders Bar to catch a ballgame on TV, shoot pool, enjoy a cold brew and a great hamburger, don't be surprised if a shadow glides by in your peripheral vision, or a spectral piano plays a tune only a ghost might appreciate. It's just part of the ambience.

SPIRITS OF THE SUMMER OF LOVE
by Elaine Ambrose

In August 1969, half a million young people traveled to a festival called Woodstock on a farm in New York. The music, mud, and mayhem from that event symbolized the Summer of Love in dramatic contrast to the national disputes over the Vietnam War. I was seventeen years old and could sing and play guitar, but was stuck in my father's potato fields in southern Idaho. The songs of that summer still echo in my head and now motivate me to tell a secret forty years later. The ghosts of Woodstock visited me in the park down in the canyon beside the Snake River. We sang their songs, and they told me their tales. Now it's time to share the story.

One of my father's one-hundred-acre potato fields in Gooding County stretched toward the horizon beyond the Snake River Canyon like a raked gauntlet of endless rows. Sweat dripped into my eyes, and my back ached as I bent to pull out another five-foot-tall sunflower. My muddy gloves strangled the stubborn weed as I swore and heaved until I fell down, pulling the plant on top of me. The dirt ball from the gnarled roots mixed with sweat on my legs and turned to mud that oozed into my work boots. Rebellious strands from my scraggly brown ponytail stuck to my cheeks, and I pushed them away with dirty hands. Because of the stifling heat, I poured my gallon jug of water over my head, and by mid-morning I was thirsty enough to drink from the brown canal that washed through the corrals and along the property.

As I worked, I imagined that somewhere beautiful girls with clear skin and shinny, blonde hair vacationed at alpine lakes or sipped cold drinks with dashing, sly men dressed in white sweaters and khaki shorts. Somewhere else, young people piled into Volkswagen vans with peace signs painted on the sides and calico curtains hanging in the windows. They drove to the city to play their guitars, sing their songs, and sell their jewelry in the park. But I didn't have that life. I was destined to spend my summers working in fields outside Wendell, Idaho, swilling dirty water from the canal, hoeing weeds from the sugar beets, and pulling giant sunflowers from the potatoes. But I had the music and it became my salvation. My prized transistor radio hung from my belt, and during that hot August of 1969, I sang along with Joan Baez, Creedence Clearwater Revival, and Janis Joplin. Working alone, I sang loud and free:

"O Lord, won't you buy me a Mercedes Benz? My friends all have Porches. I must make amends!"

That "hippie music" wasn't allowed in my parents' house, so I stocked up on batteries and played my radio outside. I could only receive two stations: KLIX in Twin Falls broadcast farm reports, Paul Harvey stories, and country music. KFXD, 130 miles away in Nampa, played my favorite songs from Santana, Creedence, and Crosby, Stills, Nash and Young. I usually kept a notebook and pencil with me so I could write poems or short stories whenever I had time. My father paid me one dollar an hour to work in the fields, and I saved the money to help pay for college. Scheduled to leave for the University of Idaho before the end of the month, I was eager for freedom but unsure about what to study. No female in my family had graduated from college. I was determined to be the first. I had good grades. My brains would help me get off the farm. That's why I never used the illegal drugs so abundant at Woodstock. But I always loved the music.

Between songs, the announcers on KFXD talked about all the drama leading up to Woodstock, and I listened to the details as I worked. The event began as a small outdoor music and arts festival organized by a group of investors who wanted to promote a few popular artists on a stage built at a dairy farm. They projected fifty-thousand people would attend. That upset local residents who wanted to ban the concerts. Signs were posted, "Stop the Hippie Music Festival." Of course, lawyers got involved and the event proceeded as scheduled. Creedence Clearwater Revival, a hot new group, was the first act to sign a contract, agreeing to play for ten-thousand dollars. Soon other popular singers and groups joined the playlist, including Arlo Guthrie, Joan Baez, the Grateful Dead, Janis Joplin, The Who, Sly and the Family Stone, Joe Cocker, and Jimi Hendrix.

This incredible lineup attracted huge crowds that no one had anticipated. Traffic came to a standstill as tens of thousands of young people descended on the farm. Then the rain came and turned the land into mud. Local authorities and event promoters had to contend with 500,000 people coping with bad weather, poor sanitation, illegal drugs, public nudity, and a delayed schedule. County officials declared a state of emergency, and the show went on for three days with relatively few catastrophes. By the end, organizers were pleased that the atmosphere prompted love and peace instead of riots and looting.

As I listened to the events described on the radio, I laughed out loud as I imagined one of my father's pastures being converted into a music festival. He would have been at the gate with his shotguns, ordering people to cut their hair, put on decent clothes, and turn down the volume. But he would have been in hog heaven with the prospect of making something big out of nothing. That was how he operated.

Monday, August 18, 1969, was the last day of Woodstock. The potato field was hotter than usual, and I tried to focus on music to take my mind off the row ahead of me.

As I worked, I sang a song that Joe Cocker had performed at Woodstock the day before.

"Oh, I get by with a little help my friends."

I worked until late afternoon and then drove the motorcycle home. I felt a strange sadness. Woodstock was over, even though I was a world away. After dinner, I sat in my room and wrote a few poems, and then fell asleep as another favorite Woodstock song meandered through my head.

"Summertime, and the livin' is easy."

The next day, my father pounded on my bedroom door at 6 a.m. "Hustle. Hustle. Time is money," he called. "You have forty acres to weed."

I pulled on my jeans, boots, and T-shirt and belted my radio. Then I grabbed a jug of water and a lunch of bread, cheese and apples, jumped on my motorcycle and headed for the field. My father had hired men to do other chores around the farms, but I always worked alone. There were no restrooms for the field hands, and that included me. At least the potato bushes provided more privacy than the beets. I worked until noon, then found a tree to sit under. Biting into my apple, I turned up the volume on the radio to hear Joan Baez singing.

"We shall overcome, we shall overcome, we shall overcome, someday."

About that time, I decided I'd had enough work for the day. Knowing I'd get into trouble, I gathered up my lunch and ran to the motorcycle. I raced down the county road hollering with delight, feeling the freedom of wind in my hair. I sped past miles of farmland dotted with workers and machinery. Everyone had the same goal: work hard and maybe the coming harvest would pay the bills. Just put your head down and keep working. But I was the brash rebel who would rather play guitar and sing my songs. I'd rather be at Woodstock.

Spirits of the Summer of Love

    I rode ten miles south of Wendell to the edge of the Snake River Canyon. I stopped at the top and looked over the vast valley stretching from Twin Falls to Hagerman. Waterfalls leaked from the sides of the basalt walls, brown rabbits scampered between the rough sagebrush over a carpet of wild flowers, and eagles flew overhead in lazy circles. The raw beauty of this rugged countryside had convinced my pioneer relatives to leave the wagon trains headed toward Oregon and homestead here. My paternal grandfather drove stagecoaches up and down the steep canyon walls, and my maternal grandfather helped build the waterways that transformed the desert into farmland. My father, once taunted for buying barren ground for twenty-five dollars an acre, introduced sprinkler pipes to the region during the 1960s and turned the ground into productive farmland worth more than two thousand dollars an acre. Forever a part of my soul, the land cradled the coffins of my relatives and produced crops that would send me to college. And, it was 2,400 miles from New York. My motorcycle wouldn't make it that far.

    I turned down the steep winding dirt road to Niagara Springs State Park. There were no guardrails on the side of the road, so I stayed near the canyon wall. The park was deserted. I edged my motorcycle onto the grass under a huge oak tree. The river splashed against the black rocks as it meandered down the canyon. Fat geese honked at me. I sat on the grass beneath the tree and immediately regretted I didn't have paper or pencil to write a poem. Nodding off, I heard the first sounds of music.

    "I see a bad moon arising. I see trouble on the way."

    The music came from a secluded spot on the riverbank. I walked over to the bushes and peered around a clump of Russian olive trees. That's when I saw them, four people sitting on logs, playing instruments and singing. I gasped as I recognized them – John Fogerty played guitar with his brother Tom. Stu Cook fingered his bass while Doug Clifford attacked his drums. Creedence Clearwater Revival performed right there next to the riverbank. I couldn't catch my breath and feared my head would explode as they finished one song and started a rousing rendition of "Proud Mary."

After the song, John set down his guitar and looked at me.

"Hey, you," he said. "Why don't you join us?"

Because there wasn't anyone else in the park, I tiptoed around the trees and moved toward the group. They stared at me with my muddy boots, disheveled hair, and messy clothes.

"You look like you went to Woodstock!" said John. "You should be happy you didn't."

"Why?" I asked, wishing I could say something more charming or at least intelligent.

"It was a mess," John said. "We didn't get on stage until three in the morning because The Grateful Dead wouldn't stop jammin'. By then everyone was asleep or passed out in the mud."

"Damned Dead," muttered Stu. "We were supposed to be the main act, and they took over."

I sat on a log beside John and decided to go along with the scenario, even though my brain told me it couldn't be true. My heart won because it encouraged me to believe in the circumstances and enjoy them. John, Doug, and Stu were only six years older than I was. And Tom was nine years older. They looked much younger than their rough images on my album covers.

"You're still the Number One group," I said. They all looked at me and nodded in agreement. "And Creedence Clearwater Revival is a much better name than the Golliwogs!"

They laughed as I reminded them of their original name.

"You play?" John asked and handed me his guitar.

"A little." I placed my fingers on the strings.

"Play an E7 chord," said Tom. "We're experimenting with a song that uses only one chord."

I played the chord and they began singing "Keep On Chooglin," a long song with one chord. I nearly levitated. I was playing with CCR. The song lasted more than nine minutes.

"You should use this to close your next show," I said.

"That's the plan," Tom said.

We played a few songs, "Born on the Bayou" and "Good Golly Miss Molly." The canyon walls echoed with the rhythms that wavered from country rock to southern jazz. The sun was disappearing by the time we stopped playing, and John began strumming "Bad Moon Rising."

"Gotta go, Sister," he said. "We got another gig down the road."

I watched in amazement as the group disappeared. Driving back, the faint headlight on my motorcycle cast eerie shadows as it bounced off the canyon walls onto the dirt road. The cool night air made me shiver and I hurried home, still breathless from my spectacular, unbelievable encounter. No one was home.

The next morning, I left early for the potato field. I wanted to work fast so I could escape again down the canyon to see if CCR would return. By late afternoon, I was on my way. In the park, I was thrilled by the raspy sound of a different voice.

"Freedom's just another word for nothing left to lose."

I eagerly hiked around the olive trees to see Janis Joplin sitting on the log by the river. She wore a long, multi-colored skirt over a red tank top with several strands of beads around her neck. I was delighted that her hair was frizzier than mine, but it suited her style. She motioned for me to come over and sit. I quickly obliged.

"You from around here?" she asked as she put down her guitar and pulled on a bottle of Southern Comfort.

"Yes," I said. "But I'm going to college in two weeks. I want to write stories and sing and play my guitar."

Janis laughed and tossed her head.

"We're all singers and dreamers, kid. I was happy being just a beatnik poet, but now I gotta go everywhere and do my thing. Sometimes I just get tired of performing." She took another drink.

"How was Woodstock?" I asked.

"Horrible," she said. "I thought it was just a simple gig but they flew me in a helicopter with Joan Baez. When I saw the huge crowd, I sort of went nuts. Then I had to wait ten hours backstage because the schedule was all screwed up. That gave me plenty of time to get wasted before I even went on. I don't remember much of anything else."

She picked up her guitar and started strumming "Ball 'n' Chain." I hummed along. By the time she lit into "Work Me, Lord" I was harmonizing with full vocals. We ended with a loud sample of "Mercedes Benz" and then she mumbled she had to go.

"Will you be back?" I asked.

"I'm not long for this earth, kid," she said. And then she was gone.

My ride back home wasn't as thrilling as the night before. I had a bad feeling about her last words, and never again prayed for a Mercedes Benz. I was beginning to think that Woodstock was not as glamorous as I had imagined. The next afternoon, I returned to the park. Gentle folk music called me to the river where I found Joan Baez. Her long hair hung in braids, and she wore a flowing flowered gown. She finished singing "Swing Low Sweet Chariot" and smiled.

"That's one of my favorite songs." I sat beside her. Meeting famous musical legends seemed common to me now, and I wasn't hesitant to begin the conversation. "How was Woodstock?"

She smiled and patted her belly. "I'm six months pregnant, and my husband's in jail, but I went anyway. My set didn't begin until one in the morning, and I was so tired. But, I was the last act of the day, and I gave the crowd some good music."

She began strumming her guitar, and we sang "Joe Hill" and "Amazing Grace." I couldn't match her lyrical vibrato, but we managed to harmonize through the verses. As we sang and swayed to the music, the river seemed to pulse in time as it surged through the canyon. A gentle breeze tickled the Aspen leaves and a flock of geese squawked overhead and flew out of sight. She stood and said it was time to go.

"Do you think I could become a singer like you?" I asked, not wanting her to leave.

With a kind gesture, Joan placed her hand on my shoulder. "You need to find your own path," she answered. "Whatever you do, you'll always be singing."

Returning home, I thought about her words—find my own path. Weeks away from going to college, I had to discover how to do it. I returned to the park several times after that, but I didn't meet any other great musical artists. No one would believe me if I told them about Creedence Clearwater Revival, Janis Joplin, and Joan Baez. But, that was OK. It was my secret.

At the University of Idaho, I majored in journalism and minored in music. I joined the concert and jazz choirs and wrote for the student newspaper. Later, my career included jobs in television, newspapers, magazines, and publishing. I wrote a few books, had some charming children, traveled the world, and always came home to Idaho. And, I kept singing. Forty years after Woodstock, I returned to Niagara State Park. I found the empty clearing down by the river where I once talked with the music legends. Faint sounds of music moved through the breeze in the canyon. I wept as I recalled the songs that shaped my youth.

"Did I do OK?" I asked to no one in particular.

The answer came, soft but clear:

"The answer my friend, is blowin' in the wind.
The answer is blowin' in the wind."

THE DOG CAME BACK
by Kathy McIntosh

Ardath Watson trotted up the stairs from the garage. She felt something brush against her bare leg and shuddered. A spider web? After all that frantic cleaning and spraying last weekend? The little buggers worked harder than she did. Idaho spiders—some as big as the famous potato.

She entered the kitchen. No welcoming aromas greeted her, and the room's silence startled her. Normally, the kitchen walls thrummed with the noise of sixties classics. The Doors would be lighting her mother's fires or worse, her mom would be crooning along with Little Surfer Girl. Mom insisted she needed the music to inspire her cooking, and usually her cooking made the aural assault bearable. Ardath rarely paused long in the kitchen in her race upstairs to change out of her work clothes and check Facebook and email. Maybe Brady had left a message.

No email from Brady. Too busy to let her know if he'd be home for their only daughter Robin's first starring role in a school play.

Puzzled about where her mother could be, Ardath wandered back downstairs to see if she'd missed a note on her way up. She knocked on the door to her mother's "granny suite" as she passed, but received no answer. She assumed Robin was still at play practice.

Maybe Mom was dropping her off at school.

"Mo-om," she called, feeling like a teenager instead of the grown mother of a fourteen year old. She headed into the family room. Everyone loved that room, a great place to cozy up and read by the fire. Her mother insisted it was because it had good feng shui.

Right.

Ardath found her mother on the floor, on hands and knees, her no-longer-taut butt high in the air, head turned to one side against the carpet. "Mom!"

Her mother held up one hand in an awkward but obvious "stop" gesture. "Hush. I'm listening."

Ardath flopped onto the leather sofa. "Not this again, Mom. Lucy is dead. She's been gone for what—more than five months now. I can sort of understand Robin's obsession because she was, after all, *her* dog, but you're not helping."

Her mother lowered her rump and spun around to face her daughter. "You are wrong on this one, Honey. I only hope your lack of faith doesn't scare poor Lucy's spirit away. We definitely need her today."

"I don't see any dog hair. She must not be here." Ardath chuckled at her joke.

Samantha glared at her daughter. The look used to petrify Ardath. It still had power, but she fought it. Ardath looked out the window. Her mother rose gracefully and sat beside her.

"I swear you are the most pragmatic woman in all of Boise. How did I raise such a cynic? I know you felt Lucy's presence here. We all did. We agreed she was happiest here with us and came back in spirit."

Ardath shook her head. "It was a joke, a way to heal after her death." She gulped air, wondering if she believed what she stated. "You said we need Lucy. What do you mean?"

"Robin's drama teacher called before you got home. Robin had a bad case of nerves today. Forgot her lines. Some of the other cast members laughed at her. Robin broke down and said her understudy could take her place."

"He just let her leave? Didn't he tell her everyone gets

The Dog Came Back

nerves?" Ardath surged to her feet. "Where is she? I'll talk to her."

Her mother stood and put a hand on Ardath's arm. "She's not home yet. And I'm not sure you're the one who should talk to her, sweetheart."

"Of course I am. I'm her mother." She snorted. "What? You want the dog to give her advice on acting? The dead dog?"

"Robin already knows everything you would say to her. She also knows that you used to be an actress and now you're a public speaker. She believes you're never afraid, never goof up."

"Nonsense. Of course I goof up. I love her."

"Yes, you do. But Robin believes her parents do everything right. You and Brady each have successful careers, yet you manage to squeeze in time to volunteer at her school and do all those good mother things. It's a hard act to follow."

"Did it ever occur to you that your advice isn't wanted? I appreciate your helping out around here, but Robin is my daughter." Ardath hated how angry she was, hated that she yelled at her mother, hated most the niggling thought that her mom might be right. She took a deep breath. "So what would Lucy do?"

Her mother smiled. "What Lucy always did. Be there. Listen. Snuggle close. Never judge."

Tears ran down Ardath's cheeks. "I miss that dog so much. She was Robin's best friend. And unlike some friends, she'd never laugh at her or go behind her back." Or be too busy with work to show up for important events in her life. "Maybe we were wrong to wait to get another dog. Robin needs her." She sniffed. "So do I."

Her mother handed her a tissue. "That, my dear, is why Lucy is still with us, in spirit. She knows we need her ...

Did Brady leave a message?"

"My dear husband is way too busy to think about his family or to consider coming home early tomorrow to see Robin in her first starring role. If, of course, the dead dog can convince her to get back on stage."

Samantha squinted at the wall clock. "I'm worried. She should be home by now."

Ardath pulled her cell phone from her pocket. "She didn't call? I'll text her."

"I called, but it goes straight to voicemail. I think she turned her phone off."

Ardath frowned and paused in her texting. "She knows better. After school, the phone comes on." She hit send. Took a breath. "So? Did Lucy tell you where Robin is? Or did the presence of a nonbeliever interrupt your séance?"

Her mother shook her head. "You *do* believe. Why is it so hard to admit it? I need to start dinner. Where do you think Robin would be?"

Ardath let out a bitter chuckle. Locked in her room, listening to *her* music while you're down here with the Kinks or The Doors, she thought. "Down by the river. Mom … you don't think she'd … kids these days, they take every little bump so seriously …"

Samantha headed for the kitchen. "Go find your daughter. And once you do, make an effort to simply listen to her. I know I had a lecture ready for every situation with you. I was wrong. Be like her dog and be her friend."

Despite concern for her daughter, Ardath laughed. "The brilliant earth mother made mistakes? I'll phone you if—*when*—I find her. She hasn't answered my text. Call me if she comes home."

Ardath trotted down the Greenbelt to Robin's school but did not find her daughter. On her return run, she stopped

The Dog Came Back

in a small clearing by the river where she knew Robin went when things weren't going her way. Since the dog had died, Ardath had worried about her daughter being alone on the Greenbelt, even though she knew it was safe during daylight hours. She didn't want to be so protective her child had no privacy. But where could she be today? Why wasn't she answering Ardath's text?

If Brady were here, he'd know where to find her. Or would he? They'd relied too long on that dog to keep their daughter company. She sat on the stone bench, elbows on knees, her head resting on her hands. "Okay, Lucy," she whispered. "Where's our girl? Where's Robin?"

Again she felt the sensation of something soft brushing against her calves. Remembered the soft plume of Lucy's tail. Ridiculous.

She jumped to her feet. "The dog park. Yes." Ardath took off running, heading south from the river on a branch of the Greenbelt that led to a small, fenced park. She found her daughter leaning against the fence, looking in. Several dogs and their owners were inside the park.

"Robin?" Ardath wanted to berate her for not checking in. She wanted to engulf her daughter in a hug that would protect her from mistakes, humiliation, and every hurt that life brought. Instead, she stood beside her little girl and noticed Robin's shoulder now stood only an inch or so lower than her own.

Robin looked up. "How'd you know I was here?"
Ardath swallowed. "Lucy."
Robin's face brightened, her eyelashes blinking back tears. "She was with me, Mom. All the way home from school. I made an ass of myself today. Quit the play. Lucy was there to keep me company. I miss her so much."

"You think she's out there playing with the other

dogs?" Ardath asked.

"Nope. She's right here with me. Like always." Robin dangled her hand to her side, as if petting her beloved pet. "I thought about jumping in the river, but she stopped me. I know you always laughed about that time I said she kept me from crossing the street in front of that fast car, but it was true. And this time, too. I felt her there, tugging at my jeans."

Ardath's heart pounded, in her throat, her ears, her legs. "You thought about jumping in the river?"

Robin rolled her eyes. "Only for a minute or two. I felt so dumb. I couldn't remember a single line. I was scared."

Ardath opened her mouth. Shut it. Put her hand gently on her daughter's shoulder.

"Do you think Mr. Flack would let me try again tonight? I hate to be a quitter."

"Ask him."

"I've got him on speed dial." Robin retrieved her phone from her backpack and turned it on. "Oops. Forgot. Sorry."

🕷 🕷 🕷

Ardath and her mother chatted with the parents of other student actors in the lobby of the school auditorium. A bell chimed. Time to take their seats. Ardath struggled to keep her expression calm.

"She'll do fine," her mother whispered.

"Yeah, I know. Lucy told you."

"Nope. Robin did."

The glass door opened. Brady looked over the heads of the audience until his eyes found Ardath's. She stiffened. Then she rushed to him, jostling a few people as she crossed the lobby.

"What changed your mind? Client cancel?" She regretted her snide remark the moment it came out.

Brady grinned. "Good shot. I deserve it." He shook his

The Dog Came Back

head. "You'll never believe what happened."

"Try me. I'll believe anything today."

Brady gave his wife an odd look. "O-kay. This morning I was coming out of my hotel, on my way to my car and the appointment with Mark at T-I."

Ardath had another twinge of guilt. She'd had no idea who Brady was meeting, or why. Next time, she'd listen.

"As I walked up to the car, a mutt ran in front of me, blocking my way. It was grinning like Lucy used to do, that silly doggy smile, and its tail wagged, so I wasn't nervous. I said something stupid like 'Hi, dog.' And then the weirdest thing happened. That little mutt gave a bow, nose on its front paws, just like Lucy. And then it ran off back to the kid calling it. And I remembered that Robin was in this play tonight, and I was going to miss it because of an appointment that I could reschedule. So I made a couple of calls and got an earlier flight and here I am. What can I say? The dog made me do it."

Ardath smiled and clutched Brady's arm. "She sure did, honey. She sure did."

HOW TO OUTSMART A GHOST
by Loy Ann Bell

My new friend Peggy and I stood on the cracked sidewalk and stared at my latest purchase—a fixer-upper on Cherry Street in Shoshone, Idaho. The house had been built in 1898, but appeared structurally sound.

"It's going to take a lot of work." Peggy shook her blonde head. "Sure you're up to it?"

"Oh, yes," I replied. "I've got a sprayer to paint the house, and I'll replace the window trims."

She stared at me. "You can paint and do carpenter stuff?"

"I've been buying places, fixing them up, and reselling them for the last thirty years."

"My late husband, bless his heart, couldn't repair *anything*," Peggy said as she surveyed the yard. "Do you know how to prune those overgrown shrubs? Look at that lawn. It's a foot high. And the cement step at the front door is crumbling."

"You haven't known me very long, Peg, but I know how to trim shrubs, and I've got a riding lawn mower. I'll build forms, mix concrete in my wheelbarrow, and put in new steps." I grinned, visualizing how the house would look when finished.

"And I 'spose you can get rid of all those weeds poking through the cracks in the sidewalks?" She pursed her lips.

"They will disappear after I spray them," I said confidently.

"My lands! You're a regular handywoman," Peg said.

"You won't recognize the place when I'm finished."

"You got it pretty cheap, didn't you?" she asked.

The house had been listed at $65,000, but had been on the market for three years. Thinking I'd have to dicker, I offered a meager $40,000, and the out-of-state owner grabbed it. The sale finalized within two weeks. "I stole it."

"*Maybe* you stole it. I've heard it's *haunted*," she whispered.

"Haunted! That's bunk. I don't believe in ghosts."

"Well, they exist," she insisted. "Just remember I warned you."

I blocked out her words. I have had a lifelong dream of retirement and creating a part-time job for myself by owning a bed and breakfast in a small town. Searching all over Idaho, I finally settled on the run-down, two-story, three-thousand-square foot home in Shoshone. After I made it beautiful, I didn't intend to move again.

"Listen, Peggy, I was an Army brat and moving became a habit. Now, for the first time in my life, I'm putting down roots. *Nothing* is going to stop me. This is my home sweet home."

As soon as she left, I headed for the kitchen to get my gloves. When I opened the back door, it squeaked. Rather, it shrieked. Loudly. I made a note to buy WD40 to get rid of the infernal noise. Grabbing a hammer and nails, I erected a sign in the front yard that announced, Sheldon House, Bed and Breakfast, Opening in Two Weeks. Excited, I stepped back and gazed at my handiwork.

That night I sat at my dressing table and brushed my hair. My mind flitted through the tasks I would tackle the next day, the first one being to mow the shaggy lawn. Suddenly, I shivered. The room felt like a walk-in freezer.

The curtains in front of the open window billowed outward. *Strange. I don't remember a breeze blowing*. I pulled the curtain aside. The leaves in the trees weren't moving. *What is going on?* I stepped back. Again, the curtain billowed outward. And I still felt *cold*. The feeling lasted another five minutes before dissipating. I wondered if my imagination had gone berserk.

The next day, I started pulling the small volunteer trees dotting the yard. I'd have to dig the larger ones, but I wanted to soak the lawn first for easier digging. I pushed my lawn mower out of the storage shed. Even riding the machine, the undertaking was laborious because of the foot-tall grass. It took three hours to mow with the blade set high. A parched, ugly brown color showed under all the hay, but it still looked better than before. I dragged out a couple of hoses and put on sprinklers to green up the lawn.

Peggy stopped by. "You're already making a dent in that yard."

We walked two blocks to the frosty stand and lapped up a couple of twist ice cream cones.

The following day, I drove to the lumberyard to purchase exterior white paint and one-by-fours in eight-foot lengths. Back home, I grabbed my hammer, pulled the antiquated trim from the windows, measured, and cut the replacement pieces. After three days, I finished nailing up the new frames, but even the unfinished brown wood improved the place.

Exhausted, I fell into bed. I'd just drifted off when the darned ceiling light flashed on. It shone directly in my face and caused me to jolt. I stumbled over to the light switch and flipped it up and down. Nothing happened. I flipped it several times. The light didn't even flicker. *Darn. Must be a short in the electrical system. It'll cost me a bunch to get that fixed.* Burying my head under the covers, I went back to sleep. The next morning, the light had gone off. I figured the bulb had burned out. I called Peggy who recommended an electrician who promised to come by at two the following afternoon.

Next morning, I ate a quick breakfast and washed my dishes. Anxious to get started on the ragged bushes, I grabbed the pruning shears from the tool shed and went to work.

Peggy called at eleven-thirty and invited me to lunch at the Manhattan, so I ran inside to take a shower. Turning on the water, I waited until it became warm and stepped in. It was freezing. Sputtering, I hopped out and gingerly tested the water with my hand. Warm. I stepped back in. Freezing. *What the heck?*

Disgusted, I quickly took a "skip bath" with a washcloth. Later at the café, I 'fessed up to Peggy about the odd happenings. She just looked at me. My mouth snapped shut like a turtle's. *Can she be right? Is there really a ghost in my house?*

Bud Ramsey, the electrician, checked the light switches and traced the live current throughout the house. Everything worked perfectly for him. I wondered if I'd lost my mind, but before he left, Bud patted me on the back and said, "Hang in there, kid. Don't let this ole house get to ya."

I finished trimming the bushes, ate clam chowder that evening and fell into bed. I don't remember my head hitting the pillow.

A noise roused me from a deep sleep. I glanced at the red numbers on the digital clock—2:44 a.m. I heard heavy footsteps clumping down the stairs. Grabbing a flashlight and my tazer from the bedstand, I ran to the door and yanked it open. A nightlight at the bend in the stairwell illuminated the area, but no one was there. Ducking back in my bedroom, I locked the door, then dived into bed and covered my head with the pillow. I didn't get to sleep again until after five.

That night I sat at my dressing table brushing my hair, glanced in the mirror, and screamed. A scowling man with long, tousled black hair, and a handlebar mustache stood directly behind me. His tattered Levis, faded blue denim work shirt, and scuffed brown boots made him look as though he'd stepped out of an old-time photo. I whipped around, my breath catching in my throat. The room was empty, but when I looked into the mirror again, his reflection stared back at me.

"Why aren't you like the others? Why don't you just *leave?*" he growled.

And leave I did, flying down the stairs as if a fire chased me. His raucous laughter pierced the air. I grabbed my cell phone, ran out the back door, and didn't stop until I'd hopped in my Buick and locked it.

I called Peggy. "Can you please come over?"

"My lands, it's eleven," she said. "Can't this wait 'til morning?"

"No, it can't." I stammered, trying to recount the events that had occurred in the house. "You were right. There's someone or *something* here." I stopped to catch my breath.

"I'll come over, but don't ask me to come in," she said. "I'll toot the horn when I get there."

When Peggy pulled up, I jumped in, and she stomped on the accelerator, nearly giving us both whiplash. "*Now* do you believe me?" she demanded.

"Yes, I do," I stated firmly.

I spent the rest of the night in her spare bedroom, and we both slept until 9 a.m. We discussed the events over coffee.

"Are you going to re-list the house?" Peg asked.

Before dropping off to sleep, I'd thought about that darned ghost and came to a decision. "Nope. I'm not giving up my dream without a humdinger of a good fight."

"But ..."

"No 'hant' is going to run me out of my house and destroy my dream."

"But how are you going to fight a ghost?"
"First, I need to know his history. How did he die?"
"What makes you think it's a *he*?"
"I saw him in the mirror, remember? And heard his awful laugh."
"I'm scared *for* you," she whispered.

We drove to the library where the librarian located an old, battered book containing newspaper clippings, and typed and handwritten stories by Shoshone citizens, from past to present. Peggy and I read each fascinating account and finally discovered what we were searching for in a yellowed newspaper clipping.

> *May 8, 1904 – Albert Robinson was found shot to death in his home on Cherry Street. Robinson was unmarried and had no known relatives. Police are making inquiries but as yet have no leads.*

I carefully extracted the next clipping.

> *July 12, 1904 – Mr. and Mrs. Norman Sackett have reported strange sounds during the night at their recently purchased house on Cherry Street. Mrs. Sackett said she is never "going to set foot in that house again" and Mr. Sackett said, "The place is haunted. We're selling."*

More clippings told of various owners who had

purchased the property through the years and concluded a ghost resided in the house. Each time they sold for less money.

"Why don't you sell?" Peggy pleaded.

"I can't," I replied. "All my money is tied up in this house, and there's no way I can sell it for what I paid."

We drove to Peggy's house where she fixed us sandwiches. As we ate, I asked, "Have you ever heard of other ghosts in town?"

"Well," she said slowly, "I've heard one lives in the old Wood River Hotel. It's been closed for years, but people claim they've seen a ghost there."

"Is he as ugly as mine?" I asked.

"Oh my, no," Peggy said. "It's a woman dressed in a beautiful blue gown."

"A lady ghost," I exclaimed. "Hummm."

"Take my advice and sell the darned house, or that ghost is going to run you crazy."

I didn't answer. After we finished eating, Peggy took me home. I'll admit I didn't feel brave when I walked into the kitchen. Sweat trickled down my neck, and my knees felt rubbery. Despite my liberal application of WD40, the door hadn't stopped squeaking. While I swept the floor, an idea began to formulate. At nine-thirty, I trudged up the stairs and sat down at my dressing table to brush my hair. This time I hoped the spectre would appear.

A few minutes later, the air turned cold and the ghost appeared. "Go 'way," he growled.

"Hey, Albert. That *is* your name, isn't it?"

"How'd *you* know?" he demanded.

"I read about you at the library," I said, more calmly than I felt. "You were shot, weren't you?"

He let out a string of expletives. "My mining partner, the dirty SOB, shot me. I haunted him 'til he died, made his life miserable, I did."

"Since he's gone, why are you still here?"

He contemplated for a moment. "This house belongs to me so I stayed."

"Don't you ever get lonesome?" I inquired.

He glared at me. "That's none of your business."

"You're right, but I just wondered if you've ever been to the old Wood River Hotel."

"What's there?"

"A lady ghost," I said. "People say she's beautiful."

His mouth fell open. "Really?"

"She wears a filmy blue dress." I set down my brush and glanced in the mirror. He'd disappeared, along with the cold air.

The next day, I related to Peggy what had happened. "I can't believe you actually talked to him," she said.

"Well, I did."

I watched for my ghost Albert every day and night for the next month, but he didn't show.

However, six months later the Realtor who had the listing on the old Wood River Hotel said he went into the deserted building to check out reports of eerie lights. After all, the electricity had been shut off for thirty-five years. Glimpsing a light in the bar area, he peeked around a corner and blinked in disbelief. Two glowing apparitions—a beautiful lady in a blue dress and a tall, black haired man—were gliding across the dance floor.

"I heard the melody, 'Beautiful Dreamer,'" he said. "Both wore radiant smiles."

LINCOLN SCHOOL'S WOMAN IN BLACK
Lincoln Elementary School, Twin Falls
by Patricia Santos Marcantonio

Working in a room at Lincoln Elementary, Joshua Crandall felt someone staring at him.

"I looked up and there was a lady all in black. She held a ruler in her hand." He returned to his task, thinking she was a teacher sent to help him. When he mentioned the woman to other school employees, he was told, "You know that is the description of the ghost."

Accounts by several people have been strikingly similar. A woman dressed in an old-fashioned long black dress with a high collar and broach. Hair in a bun. Employees call the spirit Beulah and suspect she belongs to an early principal at the school, which dates back to 1907—one of the earliest in Twin Falls.

The vision is not the only strange occurrence reported by employees, say Crandall and Principal Beth Olmstead. Drinking fountains and computers turn on by themselves; cold spots and unexplained movements show up; the sounds of kids laughing and running in the halls, and of desks being moved when everyone has gone home, all in the part of the building where the former principal had her office, now rebuilt as K Hall.

One story gives Olmstead the chills. A cook brought her young son with her one day. He played in the cafeteria with his cars while she was in the kitchen. The cook heard him talking to someone and later asked who it was. The boy replied, "That nice lady was playing cars with me, the one who wore that black dress."

Crandall says the unexplained has become part of school life and is not threatening.

And if the spirit walking the halls of Lincoln Elementary is indeed that of a former principal, she is just continuing to do her job, Olmstead says. "I think she's really taking care of the school."

LINGERING IN SILVER CITY
by Bonnie Dodge

His name was Charles Benson and I didn't like him. Not that I had much say in the matter considering I was well on my way to spinsterhood. Father said it was because my hands were big like a man's, not dainty and pretty. Mother said it was because I spoke too much instead of listening. Truth is, I was picky, dreaming of the perfect husband who would take notice of my sketches and help carry the laundry in when it started to rain. There weren't any men like that in the small town of Albany where we lived. There weren't any men who wanted my hand in marriage. Until Charles Benson came to town.

His clothes were clean, but he wasn't what you would call a dandy. His hair was blond, not dark like mine, and his hands looked like they were accustomed to working ledgers instead of plowing fields or working in the coal mines like my father's. We met one day at church, and his story was rather sad. He was on his way west to work in the gold fields when his wife died, leaving him a widower with a small baby to raise. He delayed his trip west just long enough to give his wife a proper burial and place an ad in our newspaper: did anyone want to adopt a small child?

He didn't have a lot to say about children, but when he talked about gold in Idaho and Oregon territories, the whole town listened. How I found myself on the end of his arm one Sunday after church is still a mystery to me. But he insisted on walking me home, and before the month was out, I had promised to travel west with him and help him raise his baby.

"Selina Emily," my mother warned. "Impromptu marriages have their merit, but this going west is something I shake my apron at. Ask him to work in the coal mines next to your father. He needn't go west to dig in the dirt."

"Leave her alone, Mother," my father insisted. "This is a great opportunity for our daughter."

So, even though I was eight years his senior with misgivings of my own, I followed Charles Benson to this ghost town called Silver City.

The town wasn't dead at first. When we arrived the city was booming. Mail wagons and stagecoaches rattled into town almost every day. Saloons never closed their doors, and a steady parade of men headed into the mountains day and night to work the mines. Charles was eager to strike it rich, but the longer we stayed in Silver City, the more restless I became. It takes more than gold to make one feel alive, especially if that person's life is filled with washing diapers, cooking meals, and chopping wood. I envied the women going off to Boise City or away to visit their mothers. I hadn't touched my mother's face since the day I left Albany. It was likely I'd never see her again since coaches and trains cost money. Charles barely eked a living from the mines, and became rather fond of cards in his leisure.

Many times I wished I were a horse or one of the mules carrying supplies to the mine, anything to get away. I longed to walk the foothills and feel the wind in my face. But I was married and had work to do.

"Selina," Charles would say, and I would have to stop my sketching or letter writing to tend to the children, mending, and dusty floors. Countless nights I fell asleep dreaming of my old home in Albany and thinking spinsterhood wasn't the worse thing that could happen to a person. Pining away in a gold camp surely had to be a much worse fate.

One day at the mercantile while I examined the tomatoes just freighted in from Boise City, I heard an unfamiliar voice ask, "Is this Silver City?"

"Yes," Mr. McCleary said. "How can I help you?"

"I hear they are opening another mine," the stranger said. "I'm looking for work."

Joe McCleary scribbled on a brown piece of paper and handed it to the stranger, who in his eagerness to leave, turned into me. The tomato I held fell to the floor with a horrible plop, spattering my shoes and staining forever the bottom of my best Sunday dress.

"Oh, no," I gasped. I had only enough money to purchase a few items, let alone pay for food we couldn't eat.

The stranger must have understood my awkward dilemma because he reached in his pocket and pulled out some coins. "Let me, Miss ..." he said as he paid for the ruined produce.

"Emily," I offered without hesitation, grateful the woolen gloves hid my chaffed hands, even though he must have thought me foolish wearing gloves in the middle of August.

"Let me, Emily." His voice became a melody playing forever in my head. "*Emily*," like a song instead of *Selina Emily* the way Charles barked my name when he needed a new button sewn on his shirt or wanted a second helping of cornbread.

Who could blame me for losing my head? This strange kind man sent tremors to my fingers. Taller than Charles with dusty brown hair and square shoulders, he looked strong enough to lift a tree. Dreaming of him made each new day something to look forward to instead of something to dread. Frequently, I would catch myself at the clothesline or in the garden with one ear bent toward the mines.

Emily, I could hear him whisper and even though he was miles away working underground, I would stop what I was doing and turn my head to listen to his voice flutter to the ground like Aspen leaves in autumn.

Emily. Never *Selina* like Charles scolded. "Selina, see to the children. Selina, the patch on my shirt needs attention." But Emily, my dear grandmother's name.

"Emily," he would whisper and I would forget the mending, children, my husband's bed, and run to where his voice beckoned. Past McCleary's Mercantile into the foothills beyond Silver City, near the stream where he promised someday a white carriage, a room at The Idanha Hotel in Boise City, lace, roses, and Sunday breakfast in bed.

"I've come to pay my bill," he said one day when I was buying thread at McCleary's.

"We'll be sorry to see you go." Joe McCleary shook his hand. "Have a safe journey."

My own hand faltered. This time it wasn't a tomato from the mercantile that burst. It was as if this strange man had handed me a live charge from the mine, spattering my heart all over my shoes, my hands, staining the ground forever. I dropped the spool of thread and fell to my knees. Please. Don't leave.

But he couldn't stay and I couldn't go. My heart, too bruised to mend, faltered, and three days later Charles buried me in this desert cemetery, our children dressed in black, huddled around my grave like orphans, where in August, the only relief from the heat is the dry dusty wind.

I'm not complaining. It could be worse. Instead of lingering on this windy hill with one ear turned toward the horizon, I could be hanging laundry or peeling potatoes. I'm rather content right where I am, waiting here for my stranger's safe and speedy return.

SARA'S HOUSE
by Cheryl Maude

The house in Hagerman stood tall, three stories of paned windows, peaked roofs, gables, a widow's walk, and a wide wrap-around porch. Victorian style—a graceful violet-gray, wild, deserted, locked in dreams of yesterday. Bless my father's great-aunt Samantha Sara Barron. I read the letter from the attorney twice. The house was described as "in considerable disrepair," and now it was mine.

I passed under an archway of oak branches, the light dappled, the sky veiled in green. Sunlight filtered in thin dusty shafts through the twisting branches. Bees humming in the tangle of brilliant green ivy beneath the cornices. A giant tree twisted up from the ground, its limbs clawing at the shuttered windows beyond the banisters.

I looked up toward the widow's walk. The bright sunlight hurt my eyes, but I saw someone stepping back from the railing, as if trying not to be seen. Placing my hand over my brow to block the sun, I searched the walk. Perhaps all I'd seen was a shadow.

I stepped onto the porch and unlocked the door, struggling to get it open, and for a moment it stuck. I wedged my tennis shoe against the threshold. There was a brief contest, but finally the door groaned open.

I crept into the house like a trespasser, inching a little as if expecting someone to step out of the shadows. Cold, dark, and musty, the air conveyed something pleasant—redolence, a stale odor of lavender. The floor creaked when I walked towards the light switch. I hoped that the power worked. It did. The gray wallpaper was faded and peeling. But the entry hall was spacious and formal. A generous staircase with a carved oak banister curved gracefully to the second floor. Large double doors trimmed with wide moldings led to rooms on either side of the entry hall, and beyond the staircase on the ground floor, the hall extended to accommodate more doors opening to other rooms.

"Oh ... you must have been something once." I whispered, surprised by the strange exhilaration inside me. This house could be made beautiful again.

I wandered upstairs and into a large bedroom. At the window, I drew back the curtains. Below me lay a tumbled stretch of neglected lawn filled with dandelions. Beyond that, a white picket fence enmeshed with wild rose bushes — green with small pink flowers, then a hilly field covered with low, grassy mounds and weathered grey stones. The house overlooked a graveyard. More than half the headstones had collapsed.

Was my great-great Aunt Sara buried there? I wasn't superstitious and certainly everybody in that graveyard had been dead so long even their dust was dust. I turned from the window and headed downstairs.

The house was eerie, but I was excited. Covered in dust were spacious rooms with high ceilings and elegant detailing. It needed work, but was livable. I'd worry about that later. For now, I needed to unpack my car and move in.

"Finally." I blew out a breath and collapsed face-first onto the fluffy purple duvet on my bed. My legs ached. Unpacking and putting away most of the things I'd been able to stuff into the car was harder than eight hours of shopping at the mall.

With the little strength I had left, I pushed myself off the bed and stood on the faded Persian rug. I pulled each corner of the duvet taunt until it was crease-free. Except for a thin layer of dust, the room was not particularly dilapidated. I wondered if someone had been keeping it up over the years.

That night I had trouble sleeping. The weather was warm and I should have been cozy in my linens and blankets, but I felt a chill. I listened to the bedside clock tick until my eyelids grew heavy.

In the middle of a deep sleep and enjoying a pleasant dream, I saw myself in a gazebo on a warm sunny day. The scent of lavender filled the air. I was crying, but I wasn't unhappy. I wanted to stay in the gazebo, but something started to pull me away from my dream. Instead of the summer of 1886, something was pulling me back to the present—a warm night in June 2011.

Fingers tightened around my neck—a broad hand crushed my throat. Desperately I fought the steely fingers and couldn't pull free. I struggled to wake, but couldn't.

A voice inside me told me to cling to my dream where I felt safer. I watched myself from a distance within my dream. I was again standing in the white gazebo. Baskets filled with colorful flowers hung at each opening. My dress looked like I'd just stepped out of an 1880s painting. I was holding a small gold locket. The man beside me wore a black flat-crowned hat. I couldn't see his face but felt the warmth of emotions. I was in love with him.

The vision faded. The fingers around my neck grew tighter. The people in my dream disappeared. I traveled through a tunnel of darkness—a sensation much like a ride on a carousel spinning too fast—and into the present.

Fingers were definitely gripping my throat. I struggled for air. When I opened my eyes, I couldn't believe what I saw.

A man leaned over me. His hands left my neck. There was an evil cast to his eyes, one of pure hate. He was transparent, a spirit. I had the sense of looking through radiant light energy because I could clearly see through him.

Leave this house!

I bolted upright, too stunned and frightened to scream.

There will be no more warnings.

The spirit's lips didn't move, but I understood.

I lunged at the apparition, wanting to drive it away. To prove it wasn't real, I swung at it. My hands passed straight through. The specter drifted into the curtains and disappeared.

My legs shook as I stood against the wall. I ran to the landing where the stairs led to the ground level. The wooden stairs creaked under each footfall. Pushing the front door open, I stepped into the night and sat on the step. The sky was full of brilliant stars. Silence surrounded me until a cricket chirped. Minutes later, I heard the sound of coyotes howling.

What had I just experienced? Common sense told me there were no such things as ghosts.

Determined, I walked back inside and checked the windows and doors. The windows could only open six inches. The front door had been bolted twice before I unlocked it. The rear door just off the kitchen was locked, and the screen door beyond was hooked from inside. Just as I had left them.

"There is nothing in this house except me." I chuckled at my fears.

🕷 🕷 🕷

For several weeks, nothing else strange occurred in Sara's house. I was beginning to think I had conjured up the apparition. No more voices. No more strange dreams. Nothing. I threw myself into writing, cleaning house, cooking, and taking long walks.

One sunny morning, the bedroom was peaceful, the television off. The French door was ajar and a breeze caused the draperies to stir. I felt a strange electric tingle in the air, as though a storm was about to break.

Sara!

A man's voice called from behind me. Frightened, I turned, clutching my hands to my chest. My heart knocked as hard as a fist on a door. There was a resonance in the air, a movement. Chills climbed my spine. My legs froze in place.

"Hello?" I whispered.

I groped for the flashlight on the bedside table, one that could also be used as a club, and concentrated on a patch of light on the floor close to me. A prism of green, blue and indigo floated towards the closet and then disappeared. Gripping the flashlight as a weapon, I stood before the closet and cautiously moved my hand to the door, then yanked it open. I tugged a beaded chain and turned on a light. Nothing. Just my clothes, purses, a backpack, a few extra sheets on the shelves. My shoes on the floor just as I'd left them.

When I had reached for the chain, two small books fell to the floor. They were dry and frail with age, leather-bound journals with long black silk markers. I picked one up and looked inside at the first page. I shivered when I saw Sara's name in her own hand. The ink had been dry for more than one hundred years, and in the top corner she had written *Samantha Sara Barron, 1886.*

Downstairs in the den, the sweet smell of lavender lingered from flowers in a vase on the old table. I sat in an armchair by the hearth, took a long sip of tea, and reminded myself to breathe. I held the leather books in my hands and hesitated. Maybe they could shed light on the history of this house, but I didn't feel right reading something so personal. Curiosity won over conscience.

I opened a book and found a small sepia photo—I gasped as I looked at my own face. I began to read.

July 2, 1886

*Charles has disappeared. All efforts to find
him have failed. I love him so dearly. The
only thing I wanted was to be his wife.*

I turned the pages, completely engaged. Sara wrote in the journal often, but not daily. Not every entry was dated.

September 7, 1886

*I am with child and cannot hide it much
longer. Charles, however much I care for
you, I must protect this baby.*

December 11, 1886

*Henry has agreed to raise the baby as his own.
He called me a common whore. His words are
bitter. He is filled with hate for me.*

December 20, 1886

*I told Henry that his brother is the baby's father.
I fear not only for my life but for my unborn child
as well. If only Charles and I could have married. I
hate the fact that Father promised my hand to Henry.*

Puzzled by what I had read, I shook my head and stared at the vase of flowers. The crystal, still dark where my quick rub with a feather duster had failed to remove years of dust, shown in the bright sunlight streaming through the window. A purple bud fell from the cluster of flowers onto the black oak table.

> *Leave this place! I will kill you. I will take you under the ground. You tramp!*

It was the same voice I'd heard earlier. I had the urge to run from the room, but didn't want to let the voice scare me away. With false courage, I waited several minutes before standing. I closed the journal and took the books with me, feeling a deep shiver as I left the room.

Afraid I might be losing my mind, I called on Dr. Collins the next day. The only doctor in Hagerman, he was also an amateur ghost hunter.

"Sounds like someone is pulling a prank on you. Do you know anyone who'd want to scare you away?" Dr. Collins asked.

"No. I called the police. They can't find anything."

He tapped his pencil on his desk. "I've seen strange things. I suspect there could be something. Even ghosts. Are you sure you want to get to the bottom of it?"

"Yes."

"I suggest you leave your house while we check for paranormal activity."

"Glad to," I said. "I don't know what is going on in Sara's house, but have no intention of returning until I figure out who or what is living there."

One month later, I reclaimed my home. Dr. Collins found out that Sara died under mysterious circumstances six months after the birth of her daughter. Her throat was bruised and appeared crushed. Six years after Sara's death, Henry's body lay at the bottom of the stairs in his home, his neck broken. Charles had returned to avenge Sara's death. Several weeks later, the child's nanny ran from the house claiming Henry's ghost swore to kill the whore's daughter and any living heir.

Dr. Collins also learned that Henry's body was buried next to Sara's in the crumbling graveyard. The doctor found a priest to pray over the graves and exorcise the house.

Confident the house was safe, I sat in front of the TV, cozy in my pajamas, a cup of tea on the table beside me, and read the rest of Sara's journal.

> *When I saw Henry Barron's mansion for the first time, I felt an inexplicable urge to command the driver to turn the coach around. The house was imposing with its gables and widow's walk. But I am a sensible pregnant girl and cannot run away. Something here truly leaves me icy. A touch of fear seems to rise from within my soul.*
>
> *November 1886*
>
> *I heard his voice behind me just before I felt a large hand on my back. Teetering at the top of the stairs, I reminded him of the child I'm carrying. The child he claims as his own. I know this baby is a girl. I shall give her my name. I will call her Sara Amanda Barron.*
>
> *He grows angrier every day. Next time he won't hesitate now that the baby is here. If he hasn't destroyed my journals, I hope*

Sara's House

someone finds them. Be warned. Leave this evil house and don't look back. If I had paid attention to my inner voice, my life would have turned out different.

Sara

I study the sepia picture I hold in my hand, Samantha Sara Barron. The face staring at me is like looking in a mirror. I am one of three generations of Barron women named Sara. I make a silent oath if I have daughters to break the tradition of naming the first girl Sara. I pray that the cursed name dies with me.

The house is full of small sounds, eerie creaks occasionally, wind blows through an open window, and there are times I feel the first Sara making sure her house and I are safe.

"Thank you," I whisper. I gently close the ancient journal.

UNSETTLED SOULS AT IDAHO CITY CEMETERY
by Patricia Santos Marcantonio

Joyce Obland is at home in old cemeteries. She has written books about them and has started a website, graves-r-us.com, dedicated to those she visited, describing grave markers to help people find family members. She also serves on the board of the Boise Basin Interpretive Association, which oversees the Idaho City Visitor's Center.

At the Idaho City Cemetery, Joyce has experienced not only history but also the unexplained. On one visit she and a friend heard footsteps in the leaves and branches breaking. "It caught us both off-guard," she said.

On another occasion, she took photos at the cemetery. Her habit is to take three shots in a row. The first photo captured the scenery. In the next is a mist and in the third, the mist is gone.

At one gravesite, an audio recorder belonging to ghost investigators picked up a voice calling the name "Elizabeth." Other ghost hunters claimed contact with the spirit of a boy.

Tales of ghosts at the cemetery are part of Idaho City lore. Several buildings remain from the days when the mining town flourished in the 1860s. With such a past, the cemetery is the perfect place for souls not at rest. For example, of the first two hundred people buried in the historic section, only twenty-eight died from natural causes. Most succumbed from murders, shootings, hangings, accidents, or other causes attesting to the rough mining life. Many of the graves are unmarked or marked UNKNOWN.

Idaho City is all about history, Joyce said.

These days, graves enclosed by weathered wooden

fences are scattered among tall pines. Trees even grow inside some of the enclosures as if fed by the dead. A place of beauty and perhaps, unsettled souls.

Joyce said, "I would love to hear their stories."

EPOCH IN A DRY AND THIRSTY LAND
by Vaughn Phelps

ACT I

The dust cloud rising in the west grows more impressive as it nears the settlement of Rock Creek. Locals take little notice, as here in the high desert of Southern Idaho, dust is something frontier people accept without acrimony.

For the tall man and small woman sitting primly on nail kegs however, this amounts to more excitement than ever found in Boston surees to which they are accustomed.

"Do dust explosions of this sort happen frequently?" they ask.

The bartender passes within shouting distance. "What, you mean this little blow? By gum, dust ain't no reason to allow nature to interfere with Saturday dances or territorial get-togethers. Whole lot less interestin' than a common fistfight."

The cloud arrives eventually at the Stricker Store—turned for the monthly event into the Rock Creek Feral Goat Castrating Contest and Social Club. As the pump organ wheezes the last chords of a tune, fiddlers slow and the bootstompers end what would never be called dancing by anyone who didn't owe them money.

Additional noise of chap slapping, creaking saddle-leather, and dust-beating Stetsons draws attention to the rough looking, tough talking trail-riding cow kickers making their way into the crowded room. The mud-encrusted, buffalo-smelling group is led by the smallest of the bunch. Howsoever the observation, this is in fact a female of the species. The mass of dark hair frames a sun-darkened oval face with wide-set depthless black eyes. Scraped clean of half an inch of mud, it might even be a pleasant face. Followed closely by the sagebrush saints, she pushes her way to the bar and throws down the double rye shot placed there for her.

Wiping her mouth with the back of her hand, she turns a dark gaze on the homesteaders as her men receive rotgut from a crock jug. The bartender refills her glass and whispers to her.

"Don't be mad, Miss Mel, but Sheriff Bonn was through here a fortnight ago and he said you was to curb the rambunctious nature of yore men."

"Did he, by chance, include me in that attack on our individual characters?"

"My guess is he meant it directly at you. He's sweet on you. Just trying to rub the rough edges offen you."

The fire in her eyes threatens the volatile nature of the whiskey.

"Don't you take up with me. I'm just statin' what everybody knows."

Her smile broadens as the dancers take their places again on the rough-planked dance floor. The fiddlers strike up another rousing tune, another typical eighteen-eighties spring evening communal gathering on the Snake River Plain.

The music ends and the dancers leave a clear path across the center on the barn-like room. This rattlesnake catching, bronc-busting, distance spitting, boiled-coffee drinking, and bear-chasing woman spots something that makes her blink.

Not fifty feet away, sitting ramrod straight is the most gorgeous man she's ever seen.

No, change that. He's more handsome than any statue in the book on ancient Greece she studied at school. He hasn't moved, so it must be one of those New York rotogravure

Epoch in a Dry and Thirsty Land

pictures she's heard of. He isn't real, much the pity.

Then he turns his head and leans to whisper to the small woman sitting beside him and Mel's amazement is renewed. It's as if her suddenly indrawn breath has completely voided the room of air. Wide-eyed, she turns to the trail foreman at her side. "Damn, Lucas, ain't he the most gorgeous thing you ever did see?"

"Now, Melanie, yore paw don't like you cussing."

"Paw ain't here an' iffin he was, he'd have to admit I'm right. Who do ya spose he is, an' what's he doin' here an' how kin I git'im?"

ACT II

The bartender whispers to the perfectly groomed lady seated beside the target of Melanie's admiration. The woman slides off her nail keg and heads toward Melanie.

"Miss Johannson? I'm the cook your father sent to Boston for. His telegram said I'd find you here and you'd arrange transportation for my son and myself."

Melanie hears the words without taking her eyes from the young man drawing light unto himself, even in this poorly lit room. He glances her way, stands and adjusts the knife-edge crease in his gabardine slacks. He's taller than the kerosene lanterns hanging from the rough timber rafters so his face is not visible, but the perfectly tailored suede jacket is stretched tight across his chest. When his long legs bring him into complete view, it's serendipity. With close-cropped golden hair and blistering blue eyes, he looks like an enlistment poster for the Prussian Army. He even has a scar that might be a dueling remembrance. Only missing is the heel-click and monocle. He bows deeply before Melanie and kisses her grimy, rein-toughened hand.

"I hope accompanying my mother to her new lodgings will not be a great inconvenience. I shall stay only long enough to see her settled."

Melanie has managed not to let her mouth hang open. Unable to form words, she makes her acquiescence with a hand flick, quickly regretting the action when she views her dirty hand and split fingernails. Not the expected grooming habits of a proper young lady. Luckily, she is saved further embarrassment when Jake, a trail hand who would willingly give his life for her, shuffles into the room. "Got the vittles loaded, Mel. 'Oughtta be getting back fore the coyotes come out ta greet us."

"We must get these nice people back to the ranch first, so unload the provisions and sweep the buckboard until it …"

The trail foreman whispers in her ear. "Wouldn't it be better to borrow Dr. Weiss's carriage?"

Her eyes sparkle. "Yes, of course, would you …?"

He's already heading for the door as Melanie turns to the waiting couple. "It will take a moment to arrange proper accommodations. Excuse me."

At the watering trough she removes as much of the road grime as she can without baptizing herself. After several minutes with no sign of the trail foreman and the surrey, her heart threatens a complete shutdown. She ponders where she can steal a buggy. Before she has time to find a bandit mask and blow the dust out of her six-shooter, the trail foreman and a tassel-bonneted buggy come into view.

Reentering the store with a much more demure step, she moves quickly to her fantasy figure's side. "We've not been properly introduced. I hope you will forgive my oversight." She slips her hand onto his rock-hard folded arm and flutters her eyes. "My name is Melanie Johannson, *Miss* Melanie Johannson."

He smiles. "Brian Roger Moore, happily at your service, *Miss* Melanie Johannson."

Jake, the trail hand, escorts the mother to the carriage and the party sets off for Lava Acres. The other trail hands are left to resume their drunken leisure.

Faux pas! Mel should have asked the mother's name. Brian will think her crude and unrefined.

The hooting of owls, scampering of foxes, howling of coyotes, odor of night-blooming jasmine, and chitter of cicadas seem to intrigue Brian. Melanie notes his every motion. She snuggles closer, affecting unfamiliarity with the discomforts of wilderness life and awe of the majesty of the wild prairie. In only three hours they approach the sage-covered rutty trail to the forty-thousand-acre ranch northeast of Shoshone, Idaho Territory.

When they arrive at the sprawling ranch house and stretch of outbuildings, Paw comes to stand under the swinging hurricane lanterns to great his guests.

ACT III

Mr. Johannson takes the hand of the new cook, helping her from the carriage. His disarming smile is seldom seen by ranch hands. He has been careful to cache it for use with his daughter.

"May I welcome you, Martha, to our humble land. I'm sure once you accustom yourself to frontier life you will love it as much as we do."

Melanie, with a proprietary hand on the arm of her inamorata, leads him to the porch stairs. "Father, I feel she will be more comfortable if her son is not made to hurry back to the cold, unfriendly East."

Mr. Johannson forces his eyes from the satin bedecked

and corseted Bostonian woman long enough to extend a well-muscled and callused hand toward her son. "Welcome. Call me Erik. Please consider this your home for as long as you care to stay."

Jake unloads the Moores' carpetbags and turns the horse around. Mr. Johannson stops him with a simple wave. "Jake, you can return the surrey to the doctor in the morning. You've had a long day."

As Mr. Johannson escorts Martha into the large welcoming parlor, something is different about him. He's keeping a secret. For a man in his mid-forties, ranch work has kept him in remarkably good physical shape. However, a common diet of well-gravied beef, mashed potatoes, and biscuits have given him a slight paunch, unnoticeable now because he's holding it in. His secret isn't long secured from his daughter.

Within the first month, the meal portions have been trimmed and include vegetables and canned fruit instead of huge slices of heavily sugared and lard-crusted pies. Without a murmur of discontent, all begin to look, feel and act more lively. Melanie attributes this to the blossoming of true love in her life. Until a letter comes for Brian. She instructs her ranch hands to seek knowledge of the contents, sender, and postmark from anyone who might have handled such a missive. Her heart sinks when she learns the correspondence is from a Miss Geniveve Abercrombie. That depression deepens when her father informs Melanie that he intends to ask for Martha's hand in marriage.

"By the way, Sheriff Bonn stopped by to call on you while you were out showing your future brother the country. I invited him to the engagement party next Saturday night," her father says.

Melanie paces the small patch of grass, unable to focus on the trivial details of life, such as eating and sleeping. Luckily, breathing is an action that requires none of her attention.

I can't shoot a sheriff and it would be unChristian-like to wish him to finish horizontal from a gunfight, but no other solution comes to mind. I can't feed him arsenic, and it probably tastes too horrid to take myself. Would serve them all right if I did, though.

Brian finishes helping the trail foreman break a Palomino stallion with such a golden coat that it reflects the smallest amount of light. He comes around the corner and sees the despondent Melanie sitting in the dirt. "Whatever could have brought a shadow to such sparkling eyes and bright smile?"

His calming words form a rope too flimsy to pull her up from the depths of depression. "The rotten old sheriff. He wants to marry me, and he's coming to the party tomorrow."

"Then there is no possibility that I might press my own case? Surely you have seen the love I have for you? You are the beautiful, charming, self-confident woman I always dreamed of finding, but never expected to exist. I had given up any possibility of finding her. There is no such woman east of the Mississippi."

"What?" The old Melanie is back. She turns toward the house.

"Where are you going? Have you no answer to my predicament?"

"Oh, *yes*, certainly *yes*, most definitely YES! But your predicament does not exist. I am yours forever and a day. I'm just going to get my gun. I need to make something very clear to a few people."

🕷 🕷 🕷

Jackson and his wife Abigail stand beside their car with New Hampshire plates. The hood is up and steam escapes.

The secretary of the Magic Valley Chamber and the

Twin Falls mayor has been listening in rapt attention.

"Wait, you mean that's exactly the way you saw it?" asks the mayor.

"Right. The radiator boiled over and we were letting it cool down. Hoping some dude would come by with spare water. We're here on vacation. What did we know about this high-desert heat? Anyway, we saw that all played out there among the sagebrush and jackrabbits. The people were so real we could've touched them," Jackson says. "It was like they were acting on a screen."

His wife, silent till now, finally lets loose. "Yeah, real like. Except you could see through them."

"But, ma'am, that is the way it happened. Sheriff Bonn came to the engagement party and learned about Melanie and Brian Moore. He killed the unarmed Moore, then Melanie returned fire, but Bonn's cocked gun went off as he fell. He never moved again, but his shot destroyed Melanie's left lung and heart. She died in her father's arms," the mayor says.

"This was back in 1889. Others have told of hearing voices, a few think they saw ghosts around here, but nobody ever saw the whole thing reenacted," the chamber secretary says.

"When we get back to New Hampshire, we'll tell folks about the performance. You Idaho people know how to put on a great show. It was spectacular."

"But, ma'am, it wasn't ..." the mayor protests.

The secretary pulls the mayor away before he can finish. "Let it go, John. The publicity will do us no harm."

DAKOTA FRANDSEN
PARANORMAL INVESTIGATOR
by Patricia Santos Marcantonio

At over six feet tall, Dakota Frandsen doesn't look sixteen years old. And, he certainly doesn't look like a seasoned paranormal investigator, but that's what he is.

Dakota's interest started at age nine during a school tour of the old Idaho State Penitentiary, a place rumored to be haunted. When he visited death row he saw a man hanging from a noose and screamed. As he looked back, the vision disappeared. Ever since, he has been trying to prove to others that there is more to life than what can be seen. He started his own investigations and his Paranormal Raider Force website, frandsenfiles.webs.com.

"I have been researching rumored ghost sightings on the Internet for a few years. Then once I realized how far I was into this, that's when I decided to become serious and actually start investigating."

Thanks in part to family gifts, Dakota has collected a night vision camcorder, motion detectors, voice recorders, and cameras. On his first investigation, he got results.

"I was just setting up and an older woman came behind me, screaming, 'Get out'. Of course, I jumped." He thought it was his grandmother, but she was on the other side of the building.

He has shot video of a ghostly face, recorded spectral voices, felt cold spots, and seen other strange sights. At first, his friends thought he had gone "psychotic."

"Once I actually started showing what I found, they thought twice about what I do."

Dakota is part of a phenomenon popular in movies and TV. He has already been interviewed on radio, stopped counting after four thousand hits on his website, and hopes to network with other paranormal investigators around the world.

"It's a great hobby," says Mom Shannon Malone. "It's a way for him to express himself."

"The one thing it has taught me is that the things in life that cannot be explained are sometimes the best things to have around," Dakota says. Namely, that people can return after death, and that makes him appreciate life.

LIVING ON THE LAKE
by Patricia Santos Marcantonio

Jack Monroe made sure he had everything he needed before locking his car. Paper. Pen. Gun.

As soon as he opened the door, he began to sweat. All the water in his body seemed to seep through his skin and evaporate. He should have come out at dusk. The artist in him wanted to depart with the setting sun. At noontime, however, fewer people would be in the park because the sun beat down.

He walked past the kiosk greeting people to Billingsley Creek State Park east of Hagerman. He did not stop to read the information about Vardis Fisher on the sign. He knew all he needed to know. That the writer had built his home with his own hands on a knoll overlooking a lake. There Fisher worked, mourned the death of his wife, and wrote. After his death and over a course of years, the land had passed into state hands.

Jack walked along Billingsley Creek, which flowed cool in the heat. The water was a green vein among the dirt and dry grasses. So inviting. Maybe, he should try drowning. Then again, he was a good swimmer and his instincts for survival might kick in.

Seagulls dove into the creek and squawked. Their noise sounded of taunts. He heard Monica's voice.

"Feelings changed." Squawk.

"You've changed." Squawk.

"Leaving you." Squawk.

Jack did not blame Monica. He had become mean and short tempered, as if she had personally sent the seventy-five-plus rejection letters on his desk and in his email.

He had changed into a human rocket searching for writing success. The trajectory was white hot and focused, and left no time for her.

The birds squawked again.

"Shut up," Jack told them.

The air cooled as he neared the remains of Vardis Fisher's two-story house built into and on top of a small rise. Jack noticed his footprints made a brief echo in the tall grass leading to the rock stairs. The house that Vardis built.

The lava rock chimney was untouched, but the rest of the house was bones and bricks. Weeds spurted through what used to be floors. Rusted nails, wires and other junk were scattered about.

"Damn vandals," Jack uttered. They had burned the place years ago. Down the knoll was a shop and garage that had escaped them, but ended up dilapidated victims of time. Still, the place exuded calm thanks to the trees, grass, and blue gem of a lake below the skeleton of the house. Peaceful, despite the fact a seventy-three-year-old Fisher died from pills and booze at his home, or so many believed.

Jack walked up to a cement pad, which he imagined had been Fisher's office. At that very spot, typewriter in front of him, maybe he had written "Mountain Man" there or "Children of God." Worked on his many other books, hundreds of columns and essays, or completed reports as head of the Federal Writers Project during the Depression.

"This is perfect." Jack planned to write a note on the paper he brought in his backpack, but confidence in his own words was as dry as the cheat grass covering the hills around the lake and home. Without a note, people would wonder and make up their own stories about him. Why he died at the same place where Vardis Fisher's life had ended.

Jack liked that.

From his pocket, Jack pulled out the gun he had bought at a pawnshop in Twin Falls a few days before. "God, this thing is heavy." The metal felt of finality.

He gained admiration for cowboys who lugged Colts and Remingtons around deserts, boomtowns, and under much worse conditions. They carried a gun to save their lives. He carried one to end his. He smiled at the irony.

The weight in his hand might not have been from the gun at all. His failure as a writer weighed heavier. For five years, he had worked on his novel. Within what he guessed was five minutes, editors, agents, and even small presses rejected it with ease and without conscience. He had put his heart into the story, even distancing Monica with his obsession.

He wanted to apologize to her, but didn't. In the end, the work he had sacrificed for had been dismissed as if it never existed. As if he had never existed.

What a fool.

Sucking what was to be a last breath, he raised the gun to his temple. In an instant, a brown Labrador jumped at his leg. The dog startled him so much he feared he might have shot off his ear instead of putting a hole in his head.

"Get down Walter." A man shouted from behind.

Jack stashed the gun in his backpack. The dog barked. Trudging up the hill, the old man wore a loose khaki shirt and pants. A large yellow straw hat with a wide black brim hid most of his face, which was creased like parched land. The man's white hair reached almost to his shoulders.

"Walter is the neighbor's dog. He loves this place." The old man scratched behind the dog's ears. "Go home now, Walter."

The brown lab rubbed against Jack's legs and ran down the hill.

"You're sweating buckets." The old man's voice sounded of farmyards, but tempered, as if he had traveled the world and read more than his share of books.

Jack wiped at his forehead with his arm. He sweated even more from his interrupted suicide. One more failure.

"Take my handkerchief." The old man removed one from his back pocket.

"Thank you. It's hotter out here than I expected." Jack wiped at his brow. When he wanted to return the white handkerchief, the man motioned for him to keep it. Jack nodded with thanks.

"Nice here, isn't it?" the old man asked.

"It is beautiful and secluded. We could be the only people on earth. That wouldn't be so bad."

"I used to think that." The old man started walking down the hill. Jack followed. "I was wrong. There is so much in this damn world."

They soon were on the shore of the lake. Up close, the water was crystal blue. Jack smiled at its clarity. "Everything is so green and thriving."

"You got a good way with words, boy."

"I wish I did. Not according to … never mind."

"Well, don't listen to people. Most times, they are full of it. You just have to listen to what's inside you. I sound like a preacher on Sunday, don't I?" The old man winked.

Kneeling down to the water, he scooped up a handful and rubbed it over his face and the back of this neck. Jack did the same. The cold water shocked his pulse. Jack walked under the shade of a tree, sat down, pulled off his shoes and socks and dipped his feet in the water. He let out an "ooooooohhh. Man does that feel good."

"Well, then I'm going to try it." The old man sat next to him.

Living on the Lake

"Are you the caretaker?" Jack said.

"After a fashion."

"What a great job."

The man grinned. "I have a great regard for plants and trees. They hold on and grow. They put up with so much abuse from the weather, from people. But they endure. I wish I had known that when I was your age. It would have saved me a whole lot of heartache."

Jack grinned. "You're not so bad with words yourself."

"Thanks, but I still think I sound like a preacher."

The men moved their feet back and forth in the water. Jack liked how the water glided through his toes. He smelled fish and sage. The coolness from the water flowed into him and pushed out the darkness. He closed his eyes. He wanted to cry with gratitude.

Pulling his feet out of the lake, the old man put on his worn boots. "I got work to do."

"Great to talk with you."

"Same here, boy. Next time, come when it's not so hot."

"Will do."

Jack waited until the man was out of sight, then threw the gun in the lake. After putting on his socks and shoes, he walked past the remains of the house.

Click, click click, click.

Jack turned to look at the ruins.

Click, click click click, click.

"A typewriter?" Jack said aloud. "You're hearing things. Too much sun."

He had left his cell phone in the car and had to hurry to catch Monica before she went to work at the hospital. Along the way, he drafted apology after apology in his head.

Walking past the kiosk leading into the park, Jack skidded to a stop on the gravel. Below the photo of a fortyish

Vardis Fisher was a photo of the writer's hat, the same one worn by the old man.

"Oh, my God." The old man must have been a relative of Fisher's. He wished he had known that. The questions he wanted to ask.

"Good afternoon."

Jack turned. Dressed in a khaki uniform, a female state park employee walked along with a shovel over her shoulder.

"Hi," Jack said. "I met the caretaker and wondered if he was related to Vardis Fisher?"

The woman scrunched up her nose. "We don't have any caretaker, just park employees."

"I mean the old man who works here."

"Sorry, there's no one like that." She walked faster. "Have a nice day."

From his pocket, Jack retrieved the white handkerchief the old man had given him. He rubbed his thumb over the embroidered initials.

VF

He should have been frightened, but all he could think about was what a good story it would make. He would write it someday, along with a rewrite of his novel.

The familiar Idaho wind tickled the leaves and grass, and tousled Jack's hair. The breeze brought the scent of fish, water, and life. If they could endure, then so could he.

A GUARDIAN GHOST
by Judy Ferro

The baby slept little through the night, and Bobbie slept less. It wasn't the baby's cries that woke her in the morning, but the silence. She saw him half awake, waving a perfect hand near his nose. Bobbie felt the heat even before she touched him. Fever.

Bobbie grabbed her clothes. She would get the baby to the doctor in spite of drifting snow and no spare tire. If only she had a phone so someone would know she was on the way ... If only their home weren't so remote ... If only Joe wasn't working double shifts ...

As the wind howled, Bobbie reached for a warm jumpsuit for the baby, and then wrapped him in the quilt her mom had pieced. She put on her parka and boots, found the car keys, and prayed the car would start in this cold. She headed to the front door.

A large woman blocked the hallway.

Bobbie knew the woman shouldn't be there, knew the impossible presence should be frightening. But she felt calm, calmer than she had during the baby's three days of sickness.

The woman looked like someone's mother—faded calico dress, rundown loafers, touch of gray in the tousled hair, and blue, caring eyes. Help had arrived.

"Honey, you don't have time to get to a doctor. Get that baby in a cold bath right now."

Bobbie unwrapped her son and placed him in a tub of cold water. He shivered and flailed, finally developing a full wail. When Bobbie lifted him out, the woman in the doorway shook her head. Bobbie put the baby back in the chilly water.

When Bobbie could stand the crying no more, she reached for her baby again. This time, the woman was nowhere to be seen. Bobbie held her naked son close and wept.

Everyone—the doctor, her mother-in-law, her aunts—assured Bobbie she'd done the right thing to put the baby in cold water. As for the large woman, hadn't Bobbie herself been running a bit of a fever?

Months later, Bobbie saw a photo in her mother-in-law's album of a tall wide woman smiling broadly and holding a baby on each hip. "That's her," Bobbie said. "The lady in the hall."

Uneasiness filled the room. Bobbie's mother-in-law broke the silence. "That's my mother, Bertha Campbell."

Bobbie stared at the picture. Before she died, her husband's grandmother had been a shriveled, white-haired woman in a wheelchair the only times they had met. "I remember Grandma Campbell, but I'd never imagined her young and strong."

The story of Bobbie's haunting is now a family legend. The youngest of Bertha Campbell's seventeen kids, Lyman Richard Campbell, had suffered brain adhesions from a high fever. Repeated seizures destroyed his brain bit by bit, eventually killing him. No one is certain what Bobbie saw. No one, however, doubts that Grandma Campbell had returned to save another child from Richard's fate.

THE SPIRITS OF STRICKER RANCH
by Sherri George

The Rock Creek valley where Herman Stricker claimed his homestead and ran his store has drawn people since prehistory. Indians fished along the creek banks, emigrants rested in the shade of the trees, and Ben Holladay chose it for a stage station. In the mid-nineteenth century a lively settlement grew up around the stage station, store, and Herman's ranch. People lived, loved, and died there, and many claim their spirits remain in the early twentieth century house and on the grounds of the Rock Creek Station and Stricker Homesite.

The first burials on site, found by researchers with cadaver dogs, are at the west edge of the orchard along the caretaker's driveway. These are believed to be the graves of travelers along the Oregon Trail. With thirty-thousand deaths along the trail in the two decades of its greatest use, no wonder some emigrants buried their dead on the banks of Rock Creek.

The pioneer cemetery a quarter mile west of the store contains graves dating from 1874 to 1897. Of the marked burials, there are three emigrants—a local woman, a freighter crushed between his wagons, a murder victim, and the horse thief William Dowdle, whose death at the Rock Creek Store Charles Walgamott recounted in his book *Six Decades Back*. The wooden markers shine against the gray soil on moonlit nights, and often shapes seem to rustle through the brush along the creek.

The Stricker family plot is in the Rock Creek Cemetery on Rock Creek Road about a mile from the house. The first of the Strickers to pass away was William Pro, who died of illness in 1893 at age two. Herman died in 1920, probably in the master bedroom. Lucy Stricker died during the hard winter of 1949 in the front bedroom now called Lucy's Room. Snow made the roads impassable, so the family laid Lucy's body out in the sitting room and closed the pocket doors. She lay there for several days, preserved by the extreme cold until the funeral home could retrieve her body.

Lucy's spirit is said to inhabit her family's homestead. People have claimed to see her looking from the downstairs windows, or felt her hand on their shoulder. Another spirit is the girl in white, who has been seen on the lawn, as well as in the house, and even at the pioneer cemetery. Sometimes she is a preteen girl, other times a young lady, but always in a long white dress in nineteenth century style. At times she appears in photos, a misty white shape not seen when the picture is taken.

Another spirit is said to linger in the upstairs hall and the Blue Bedroom of the Stricker house. A psychic told one of the descendants that Roland, one of the Stricker sons, remained in the house. He served in World War I and made his living as a cowboy, dying in 1969. Perhaps the peace of his earthly home drew him back.

Strange creaks and rattles disturb the house now and then, and low voices echo from the creek bank, the words unclear. On still nights, the sounds of hoofbeats and turning wheels arise from the still-visible roadbed of the Oregon Trail/Kelton Road. Lights seem to flicker in the old store building and the cellars, only to extinguish when someone approaches. The rustle of cards and the click of poker chips might be heard, but the dead do not deal the living in.

Paranormal investigators have set up their equipment across the site, but on those nights otherworldly activity failed to manifest. Many people have feelings of being watched, or walking through cold spots. Eyes in portraits lining the walls often seem to follow observers, and the baseboard heat is unreliable at best on cold days.

A place haunts a person in many ways, and everyone's experience of the Rock Creek Station and Stricker Homesite is different. Who can say if the Stricker Ranch haunts the spirits of the dead as it does those of the living?

WHERE GO THE GHOSTS?
by Bonnie Dodge

If ghosts could talk, what would they say
when moonlight chills the air
in secret rooms with hidden locks
when no one else is there?

If ghosts could walk, would they go far
enough out of their way
to creep behind a bedroom door
as naughty children pray?

If ghosts could cry, do you suppose
their tears would be unclear
pale puffs of frost that slowly die
when evil spirits near?

If ghosts could die, would that imply
a sempiternal woe,
sad faceless shadows lost at night,
Wherever would they go?

ABOUT THE AUTHORS

ELAINE AMBROSE left the family potato farm outside Wendell to travel the world, write and publish books, raise a family, and sing in the rain. She is the author of several books, owner of Mill Park Publishing in Eagle, Idaho, and organizes "Write by the River" writers retreats. Find more details at her website, www.ElaineAmbrose.com.

LOYD BAKEWELL, a retired mailman, resides in Twin Falls, Idaho, with his wife Ruth. He has forty-two foster children and three of his own. He serves as an aftercare chaplain for men in Twin Falls and Jerome halfway houses. His writing has appeared in magazines, newspapers, and poetry anthologies. His essay won the George Washington Medal of Honor from the Freedoms Foundation. He has also compiled a memoir, Journey to Manhood, to be published.

LOY ANN BELL has had articles published in horse magazines in the U.S. and England, and has been a reporter for Twin Falls, Jerome, and California newspapers, and the Western Livestock Journal. She won the prestigious Author Mania Contest in Texas, placed in *Idaho Magazine*'s Fiction Contest, and been a consistent winner in Idaho Writer's League contests. A former IWL State President, her collection, *Short Story Mysteries: With a Western Flavor (Volume 1)* was published in 2012.

ANDREW W. BLACK was born in the Jerome area and graduated from the Valley School District. He has a passion for learning, reading, and writing. He is also an avid outdoorsman and gets much of his inspiration from the backcountries

About the Authors

of the Gem State. He often finds the best time to jot down ideas is while fishing or camping with his beloved family. H. P. Lovecraft, Robert E. Howard, and Michael Crichton are among his favorite writers.

BILL COPE lives in Meridian, Idaho, within two miles of where he was born and raised. A musician by education, he has played professionally since attending the University of Idaho where he was also introduced to creative writing. Since 1996, he has written a regular political/humor column for the *Boise Weekly*. For almost forty years, Cope has been married to Rebeca, who he met while living in Ohio. They have two grown daughters.

EILEEN L. DAVIDSON lives with her furry family in a sixty-seven-year-old farmhouse. When she moved in, there were six apricot trees in the backyard and a basement fruit room with a dried rose left on one shelf. She has been writing seriously for six years, edited an anthology for the Caldwell Chapter of the Idaho Writer's League, and has had two other short stories published.

BONNIE DODGE is co-author of the anthology, *Voices from the Snake River Plain* and author of *Miracles in the Desert, a book of essays about Twin Falls, Idaho*. Her column, "Life in this Magic Valley" ran in *Ag Weekly*, a supplement to *The Times-News* for six years. Idaho Writer's League's 2010 Writer of the Year, her work has appeared in I*daho Magazine, Sun Valley Magazine*, and *Rawhide & Lace*. Her book *Waiting* will be published in 2014 by Booktrope. Her website is bonniedodge.com.

CONDA DOUGLAS, a fifth-generation Idaho native, delights in writing about a fictionalized version of her

About the Authors

hometown, Sun Valley. Fictionalized, she says, so that her friends and family avoid pointing out her less-than-perfect, okay wretched, memory. More adventures in Starke appear in her mystery series, *Starke Naked Dead*. Visit her blog at condascreativecenter.blogspot.com.

JUDY FERRO is a member of an Idaho family of readers, teachers, and storytellers. She is the author of *Desiderata and Agnes*, the first two books in her *Karolus Chronicles*. She loves history and historical fiction. Visit her at judyferro.com or her Facebook page at facebook.com/judyferroauthor.

KARMA METZLER FITZGERALD writes from her home, the Queendom of Karmalot, near Shoshone, Idaho. When not wasting time on Facebook, she writes essays and features, typically about friends and fellow dairy families. She also spends a lot of time driving children to various events, including towing a trailer full of 4H and FFA animals, and praying she doesn't have to back up. Follow her wanderings at adventuresinkarmalot.blogspot.com.

SHERRI GEORGE was born on the edge of a canyon in Twin Falls, Idaho, and grew up on a chinchilla ranch in Mountain Home. She has written fiction since she could hold a pencil and is the winner of numerous awards, including first place in the Idaho Writer's League Novel Contest and *Idaho Magazine's* fiction contest. Her work has appeared in *Catholic Digest, Idaho Magazine, Habibi, Jareeda*, and special interest newsletters. A medical records director by day and a belly dancer for fun, she counts writing historical novels her life's work.

LINDA HELMS has been writing since high school. A twenty-year plus member of the Idaho Writer's League, her fiction and nonfiction has won several awards and has appeared in *Idaho Magazine*. She writes the Jerome County Historical Society monthly newsletter and wrote a Jerome pictorial history book for Arcadia Publishing's Images of America series.

GISELLE JEFFRIES graduated from Boise State University with a major in English writing and minor in Spanish. She is published in *An Eclectic Collage: Creative Works by the Women of the Pixie Chicks Writers' Group* and *An Eclectic Collage Vol II: Relationships of Life: More Creative Works from the Women of the Pixie Chicks Writers' Group*. She also released *Thoughts of Poetry*.

GROVE KOGER, a Boise librarian, is author of a play, *Ruby Testifies*; a travel narratives guide, *When the Going Was Good*; numerous articles in Boise and McCall magazines; and short fiction in *Lonesome Fowl, Bewildering Stories, Absinthe Revival,* and *MicroHorror*. His essays on haunted houses and homunculi appeared in the *Ashgate Encyclopedia of Literary and Cinematic Monsters*. He is married to writer Margaret Koger.

MARGARET KOGER of Boise is an Idaho native who grew up on a small farm near Homedale. Sunday excursions often took her family into the heart of Owyhee County where stories set in ghost towns and abandoned mines dramatized the settlers' struggles for survival. A school media specialist, she has published in *Avocet, Montucky, Eternal Haunted Summer,* and *Mouse Tale Press*.

PATRICIA SANTOS MARCANTONIO is the author of the award winning *Red Ridin' in the Hood*. She co-authored the anthology, *Voices from the Snake River Plain*, and has been honored for her journalism, screenplays, and short films. The Magic Valley Arts Council produced, *Tears for Llorona*, her first play. Her novel, *The Weeping Woman*, was published by Sunbury Press, which will release her new book, *The Ghost Sisters and the Girl in Hallway B*. Her website is patriciasantosmarcantonio.com

CHERYL MAUDE, an Idaho native, lived in Hagerman for twenty years. She graduated from Boise State University with a marketing degree. She lives in Caldwell, Idaho, with husband Doug and the enduring spirits of her four poodles on a private lake. In the summer she and husband enjoy a glass of wine while watching their black swan swim.

SHERRY SCHUBERT MCALLISTER grew up in Pocatello, Idaho, a member of an ISU faculty family. After graduating from UC Berkeley, she hitchhiked across Europe and returned to Twin Falls to raise a family and teach teenagers to solve quadratic equations. She has two published novels, *Puffin Island* and *Celtic Compass, Part I*, with *Celtic Compass, Part II*, published in 2012. She has received awards from the Idaho Writer's League and *Idaho Magazine*. Visit her at sites.google.com/site/sherryschubert11.

KATHY MCINTOSH, a professional editor, lives and laughs in Boise. She writes a biweekly column on business writing for the Idaho Statesman's Business Insider magazine. Her novel, *Mustard's Last Stand*, released from L&L Dreamspell, was chosen one of Idaho's Top Ten Fiction Books of 2013 by Top Idaho Author and Book Awards, which also selected her as one of the top three new fiction authors of 2013. See more at: kathymcintosh.com.

About the Authors

JAY MICHAELS is a radio and TV broadcasting veteran of more than thirty years at several stations, including thirteen years as a general assignment reporter at KMVT-TV. He is surrounded by a houseful of women of varying ages, the reality of which is a far cry from 1950s science fiction movies in which intrepid male astronauts are, "Trapped! TRAPPED! On the Planet of WOMEN!" He is intermittently seen in the company of various musical instruments, the people who wield them, and the occasional model rocket.

W. LENORE MOBLEY is an Idaho native who enjoys writing short stories, particularly about the state and women who enjoy riding horses there. She is author of five *Journey Series* books. The final one in the series, *The Journey Home*, was published in 2012. Her most recent nonfiction work is *Women and Their Horses Along the Snake River Plain (Enjoy the Journey)*. She bids all a happy trails.

VAUGHN PHELPS has written four novels, four TV episodes, twenty-three screenplays, and hundreds of short stories. When he moved from California, he didn't have to guide an oxen-powered covered wagon through rutted, muddy tracks, but most of his short stories didn't survive the trip, suffering in the translation from Apple IIGS to IBM format. He began devoting more time to short stories. The result is five volumes—the first two produced and the other three are ready to go. He was named the Idaho Writer's League Writer of the Year in 2013.

JO ANN ROBBINS has retired to her grandfather's farm in southern Idaho where she was raised. She spent her career in research and education at Washington State University and the University of Idaho. She now raises ornamentals,

About the Authors

fruits, vegetables, and chickens for egg production and is a UI Master Gardener and Food Safety Advisor. The time to reflect on a lifetime of interesting experiences has spawned a hobby of writing with the desire to inform and entertain.

CATHY WILSON is a Buhl School District substitute teacher. Her articles have appeared in *Woman's Day*, *True Story*, and *Fate*. She has won prizes, including ghost-hunting equipment, for her essays and humorous poems. Her poetry received honorable mention from the League of Utah Writers. In 2011, she published her first book, *STRANGE Unexplained Tales from Idaho and Beyond*.

NADINE YORK lives in Boise where she relishes the pursuit of haunts, mysteries, and secrets — the stories embedded in the everyday lives of ordinary humans.

PHOTO CREDITS

CAVE MOUTH - Patricia Santos Marcantonio	vi
UNIVERSITY INN, GOODING, IDAHO – Patricia Santos Marcantonio	8
REST STOP – Patricia Santos Marcantonio	18
OLD HOUSE – Lebbie Martin	28
SHOSHONE INDIAN ICE CAVES - Fred Cheslik	36
OLD BED FRAME – Bonnie Dodge	48
PETROGLYPH - Bonnie Dodge	52
BOOT AND HAT – Bonnie Dodge	64
SNAKE RIVER CANYON – Patricia Santos Marcantonio	68
HAUNTED SWING SET - Bonnie Dodge	76
ROOM NO. 10 SOLOAGA HOUSE – Bonnie Dodge	90
FULL MOON OVER TREES – Bonnie Dodge	104
SIBERIA AT OLD IDAHO PENITENTIARY – Bonnie Dodge	108
SCHUBERT THEATER, GOODING - Charmianne LeaVell	112
OLD SHOES AT TWIN FALLS COUNTY HISTORICAL MUSEUM - Patricia Santos Marcantonio	118
PAST IN THE MIRROR - Patricia Santos Marcantonio	132
WATER BABY - Bonnie Dodge	142
PIECES OF HEAVEN CUPCAKERY - Bonnie Dodge	157
TWIN FALLS PUBLIC LIBRARY – Patricia Marcantonio	160
TWIN FALLS COUNTY HISTORICAL MUSEUM DISPLAY - Patricia Santos Marcantonio	162
ANGEL – Patricia Santos Marcantonio	172
OLD PHOTO FROM SIDEWINDERS BAR – Patricia Santos Marcantonio	178
LINCOLN ELEMENTARY – Patricia Santos Marcantonio	208
IDAHO CITY CEMETERY – Patricia Santos Marcantonio	212
OLD HOUSE – Anonymous	218
IDAHO CITY CEMETERY – Bonnie Dodge	228
STRICKER RANCH – Bonnie Dodge	232
LAKE AT BILLINGSLEY CREEK STATE PARK - Patricia Santos Marcantonio	244
STRICKER FAMILY – Idaho State Historical Society	254
GHOSTLY TREES – Patricia Santos Marcantonio	258
COVER PHOTOS - Bonnie Dodge and Patricia Santos Marcantonio	

Made in the USA
San Bernardino, CA
07 March 2020